IN THIS VOID

A NOVEL

IN THIS VOID

A NOVEL
BY ALEX RASMUSSEN

SUMMER 2025

CHIN MUSIC PRESS

SEATTLE

PUBLISHER:
Chin Music Press
1501 Pike Place #329
Seattle, WA 98101-1542
USA
www.chinmusicpress.com

All Rights Reserved
ISBN 978-1-63405-083-8
First {1} Edition
COVER PHOTO: Travis Tyler
COVER DESIGN: Ashley Zuckerberg & Sara Camille
Printed in the USA
LIBRARY OF CONGRESS CONTROL NUMBER: 2025930145

For Sonja
and her deep knowing

Advance Praise for *In This Void*

A lyrical live-in journey that slams the reader in the back of the tour bus, hollers at 'em to carry the amp, and makes no apologies for THE behind the curtain tour. This dip into musical madness is a wild ride.
—Ashley Erwin, author of *Grit Black Blood*

Alex Rasmussen delivers a raw and lyrical tale of desperate men and women. Part Nashville, part Easy Rider, In This Void is exhilarating honkytonk noir.
—Sam Wiebe, award-winning author of *The Last Exile*

The first thing Kody noticed about the woman was the hypnotic sway of her wide hips, hugged by a fire-engine red miniskirt that climbed higher with each stilettoed step across the sun-soaked sidewalk. She looked like one of the dancers in the hip-hop videos he'd often watch on the basement TV before school—those scantily clad seductresses who would make his guts go molten and drain waistward until his skin could barely hold the impossible pressure.

The woman waved with her fingers at Kody, seated in the back of the sedan, and Grandma scoffed from the driver's seat, shaking her head and glaring at him in the mirror.

"That is *not* a lady, Kody." Paper-thin brake pads squealed in pain as Grandma eased into the turn lane and mumbled, "Tramp."

Digital numbers on the dash read 3:22. At this time a month ago, Kody would've been riding the bus home, dreading the moment when he would have to open his front door. Now, on summer break, a similar foreboding clung to him like the cigarette stink that would linger after the nights when he'd be forced to stay up until 4:00 a.m. playing video games. The following day, classmates would conspicuously inch their seats away from him.

Grandma's car crept into the parking lot of a squalid, three-story motel and slowed to a stop. A bathrobed woman leaning on the second-floor railing lifted a joint to her lips and narrowed her eyes at the vehicle.

"Do I have to?" Kody pleaded.

Grandma's reply was as stern as a death-sentence gavel. "He's your father."

With his electric guitar in a bag on his back, the wiry Kody carried his small amplifier up the stairs to room 207. He knocked, and Father's voice called out from the other side of the door. "Kody!"

"Yes."

"Kody, get your ass in here."

The shades were drawn, and except for the muted television's cold blue light, the room was dark. Empty bottles were cluttered atop the bureau. On the bed, Father sat shirtless with his back against the headboard; his pale belly hung over the edge of the blanket. With the television reflecting in his thick glasses, he said, "Sit dooown," in an airy tone, as if coaxing a cat.

Kody closed the door, removed his guitar bag, and leaned it against the wall. He laid the amp on the carpet and sat in a chair that reeked of Marlboro smoke. Balled-up tissues were strewn about the bed, the nightstand, the carpet.

"Well," Father said. "What's, uh ..." He smirked. "What's up, Doc?"

Kody forced himself to laugh.

"You know who says that?" Father asked.

"Bugs Bunny."

"That's right, Bugs Bunny," Father replied. "You used to love those cartoons. When you were a *little* punk." His voice softened. "Now look at you." He leered through hollow eyes. "Do it!" He cackled. "Look at yourself."

Traffic sped by on the highway, and Kody wished he were out there, in some truck headed forever away.

"You're a man now, Kody. All grow'd up." Father ran a hand through his greasy hair. "How'd you do that? How'd you get so big?" He reached beneath the blanket. "You used to live in my balls, you know."

Kody dropped his gaze, focusing on the carpet.

"Oh, come on," Father said. "Don't be such a wuss." He raised his hands as if under arrest. "I'm only kidding." He tilted his head. "What? You gonna tell Mommy?" He grabbed a bottle from the nightstand and took a swig. "Sue me."

On the silent television screen, two people were talking, and Kody could see that they were trying to be funny. He watched with tunnel-visioned intent, hoping the humor would reach into the room and rescue him. Father watched too, clutching his beer. After a long nothingness, Father's eyes began to water, and a dull groan rose from the depths of his gut. Fighting the emotional onslaught, he barked, "Ack!" and lifted the bottle to his mouth, draining the contents before tossing it onto the carpet. He snatched another bottle from the nightstand and opened it with a lighter. "Don't ever take that first drink, Kody." He sucked the beer and swallowed, focusing on the TV. "Don't you ever take that first drink."

"Okay."

As Father stared at the screen, a tear slid down his florid cheek. He set the bottle on the blanket and began to sob quietly. With each muffled whimper, Father's shoulders bounced. He removed his glasses and held a palm across his eyes. The bottle toppled over. Pilsner puddled on the bed.

Knowing his role, Kody plugged his amplifier into the grime-caked socket and removed his guitar from the bag. He connected the cable and pressed the power button. As Father wept, Kody played a series of slow, finger-picked chords, focusing his weathered attention on each note. He needed to sing well; needed to be a good son.

"My child arrived just the other day. He came to the world in the usual way ..."

Kody's hands trembled as he navigated the rusty strings. His voice slipped in and out of pitch.

"And he was talking 'fore I knew it, and as he grew, he'd say,
'I'm gonna be like you, Dad.
You know I'm gonna be like you.'"

Kody closed his eyes. No motel. No empty bottles.

"Oh, the cat's in the cradle and the silver spoon.

Little boy blue, and the man in the moon.

'When you comin' home, Dad?' 'I don't know when ...'"

The music carried Kody to a place beyond life, and he fantasized about staying in that painless void forever. Soon, though, the song was finished, and he sheepishly returned to reality, where Father was staring at him. His eyes were puffy and bloodshot, but he had stopped crying.

I

The Compass Points South

Sunlight blazed through the bedroom window and burned Kody's eyelids open. Groaning, he shifted between the sheets, hiding his head in a shadow. His bare back was sweaty from pressing against the girl's while they'd slept. She shifted too, yawning sweetly the way a small furry creature might. Kody checked his phone: thirty minutes before his alarm was set to go off. Not enough time for another sleep cycle, but more than enough to finish what the lazy nails tracing his spine were starting.

The walk from the girl's apartment to Kody's van seemed longer than it had the night before. Everything about this day—as he'd be running on only a few hours of half-sleep—would likely drag along. He might be able to catch a nap somewhere along the highway if he made good time.

After climbing into the driver's seat and starting the engine, Kody fished dollar-store sunglasses from the glove compartment and slid them over his aching eyes. The thrill of conquest simmered somewhere beyond the fog of fatigue, and he tilted the rearview mirror so he could see himself, ruffling fingers through his matted brown hair. Raising his chin, he poked at the pale skin near his neck tattoo, where the girl's teeth had left red marks.

Once he'd reset the mirror, he checked his phone. There were some junk emails and a message from Red.

Darcy's on board for the session.

A dull jolt quivered Kody's insides as he pictured himself in the recording studio with Darcy, one of Nashville's most acclaimed drummers. He imagined standing in the foam-padded vocal booth, strumming his guitar and surging with pride as he watched her through the window, playing along to his music. Moments later, he was hanging his head after botching a chord change, forcing the entire band of top-tier musicians to restart the song yet again.

Red, Music City's most influential producer, addressed Kody through the headphones. "You'd think that since you wrote the tune, you'd be able to play it."

The mechanized growl of a passing garbage truck returned Kody to the present, and he replied to the text, *Cool,* before putting the van into gear.

Interstate 90. Headed east.

The drive from Seattle to Boise usually took about eight hours. Factoring in the time zone change, Kody would arrive at the gig just in time to assemble his sound system, warm up his voice, and start his three-hour set. Unless he drove a hundred miles per hour, a nap would be out of the question.

"The price I pay." He shook his heavy head and took a drag of his cigarette.

The smoke seared his lungs, and he held it for a moment before exhaling into the highway *whoosh* of the cracked window.

As it tended to on long drives, Kody's mind wandered. He recalled some potent details from his night with the girl: the way her jade-colored eyes had rolled back as she bit her lip and clawed at the pillow above her; a midnight walk through the woods, each of them clutching a bottle of beer in one hand and their clothes in the other; her full lips curling slowly upward when Kody's words stirred something within.

Recalling a statement she'd made, he repeated his response. "But we *are* animals." He stuffed the cigarette butt into an empty soda can in the center console.

The girl had been charmingly uninhibited, intensely curious. Lying in bed, she'd curled into him and dragged painted claws from his chest downward, asking, "So you quit your job *how* long ago?"

"About six months."

"And this is all you've been doing since?"

"All I've been doing?"

She propped herself up on an elbow. "Yeah. Playing at pubs, going home with the bartenders."

"My goal is every bartender in the country by next year."

She cocked her head, scanning him with a smirk. "Well, with how quickly you finished, I think that's doable."

There'd been no exchange of phone numbers or social media profiles, only of sarcastic banter and bodily fluids; a late-night rhythm that was becoming as routine as the Caravan's tank of gas every couple hundred miles. And, as predictably as the fuel soon running dry, the fragmented memory of this girl and her charms would fade gradually into the rearview like everything else in his transient life.

"When they're whipping past at eighty miles-per-hour, you can't see the chips in the paint."

The van told Kody he should write that down, *"Could be a good lyric."* Steering with his knee, he fished the notebook and pen from the glovebox and scribbled the sentence. Then he tucked both into the center console beside the soda can. Before the van had a chance to criticize his handwriting, Kody reached for the radio dial.

"Security-camera footage showed four teens lifting the deer carcass from the back of a pickup truck into a shopping cart before pushing it through the open doors of a supermarket."

The radio host's voice crackled with static as the old motor labored up the hill that split the craggy peaks of Snoqualmie Pass. After several piston-pumping minutes, the van reached the summit, and the road leveled out, winding between towering evergreens and patches of melting snow. Kody rubbed his palm back and forth across the dash as if he were petting the belly of a two-ton puppy.

Tail wagging, the Caravan hummed along.

"What's the cage for?"

The man who had asked the question stared at Kody with beady eyes shaded by the brim of a faded baseball cap. With one hand, the man pumped gas into his ramshackle pickup; the other clutched a half-eaten microwave burrito. "You got an animal or somethin'?"

Appraising the man, Kody knocked on the van's back window. "For the hostages."

The man laughed nervously, but when Kody's expression remained straight, he adjusted his cap and glanced at his feet, lifting the burrito toward his mouth. Kody recognized the soft sadness that washed over the man. He'd seen it many times after denying people the connection they desired. It reminded Kody of the way a child might react if, after asking his mother for a hug, the mother had said, "No."

He indulged the man. "I got it at a government auction. The post office was selling a bunch of them with almost no miles on the engines."

A fleck of burrito took flight as the guy sprung to conversational life. "I 'member seeing these around a few years back. Don't see 'em any more." He waddled toward the white Caravan and peered in the rear window. "You got a mattress in there and everything."

Kody nodded. "I play music, so my stuff's up under the bed frame. Speakers, stands, cables, my guitar."

"You'd never know it from this angle." The man took another bite, chewing as he continued. "And even if you *could* see the equipment, good luck getting at it through that mail cage." He chuckled. " 'less you had a pair of bolt cutters!"

"That's the idea."

Kody was never good at ending these meaningless interactions. Luckily, the man seemed to sense that they'd reached their conversational threshold. "Welp." He wiped his mouth and brushed his hand on his jeans. "Hope them hostages don't escape on 'ya!"

Kody couldn't muster a laugh, or even a smile, and the glimmer extinguished from the man's eyes before he wheeled around and returned to his pickup.

With his hands in the pockets of a long black coat, Kody turned to gaze beyond his van, into the distance, allowing himself to become hypnotized by the contoured cloud shadows that crept across the golden hills. As he noted their resemblance to massive black slugs, the Feeling began to emerge, cold and insistent as it often was, expanding in his gut. He could never fully place the sensation, which morphed and twisted with time. Here, it was accompanied by a memory from years ago: clutching the straps of her backpack, she shot an anticipatory glance over her shoulder as she hiked toward the river with Kody close behind. Those eyes had seen the world with fearless amazement—with loving wonder—but when they focused on Kody, he hid from their warmth, turning inward like a flower wilting. He wondered where she might be at that moment.

Whose life is she making perfect?

Before he could further converse with his phantom companion, the gas pump clicked to a stop, and the man's truck sputtered as it lumbered away from the station.

Some people applauded. Others nodded in approval, chewing burgers or salads. A table of five, near the back of the patio, continued their noisy conversation. With a sigh, Kody glanced at the time on his phone: 8:13. Less than an hour left in his set.

"Thanks." He addressed the dinner crowd from a pint-sized stage in the corner, sliding his phone into his pocket. "Here's one of my own songs now."

While strumming chords he'd spent hours selecting and arranging, a motorcycle roared past on the nearby road. Kody tightened his grip on the guitar's neck and glared at the Harley as it barreled toward a distant intersection. The cable-suspended traffic signal swayed in the breeze as he imagined an SUV running the light, sending the motorcycle bouncing across the pavement like a metallic tumbleweed. The wailing of sirens would follow …

Returning his attention to the music, Kody began singing lyrics— painstakingly crafted from the raw materials of experience and emotion—to a patio alive with laughter and conversation. Shaking the mounting insecurity, he played on as he always did, closing his eyes and imagining an audience who cared.

When the gig was over, he sat at the bar with his notebook and a beer. As people chatted around him—joking, telling stories, and so on—he took inventory of moments during his set when he had been off pitch and lyrics he'd forgotten. Notes he would study before the next performance.

"Writing a new song?" a gentle voice asked.

Pretending not to hear, Kody focused on the pen while the girl climbed onto the barstool beside him. Folding her arms on the counter, she leaned to get a better look at what he was writing and began to sing in a soft and playful tone: "Cute girl in a Boise bar."

Kody felt a tingling in his core and recognized the sensation as a laugh trying to bubble up from inside. He stifled it, concentrating on his notes.

High F in the last chorus of "No Woman, No Cry."

The girl sang another line. "I tried to ignore her, but she was a great sing-*gar*."

Kody released a chuckle that sounded as if he'd been slugged in the gut—a forceful "Ha!" followed by the turning of his head to meet the girl's inquisitive, sparkling eyes.

She smiled proudly and straightened her posture. "Gotcha."

Allowing one side of his mouth to creep upward, Kody maintained eye contact. "You did." He scanned the girl's face and found no fear. "You should have come up and done a song with me."

The girl shrugged. "Maybe next time." She flicked the zipper on Kody's guitar bag, propped against the bar between them.

"Tomorrow then. In Salt Lake City."

The girl shook her head. "Don't think my job would like that too much."

"You won't need a job when you're a roving singer."

She smirked. "Is that what you call yourself? A *roving* singer?"

"It's what I am."

The bartender came out from the kitchen and asked the girl what she wanted to drink. As she ordered, Kody watched, intrigued by her playful nature. He glanced down at a large and colorful tattoo—a bouquet of assorted flowers—peeking out from beneath a pair of jean shorts. His gaze lingered on the smoothness of her skin.

The bartender poured Kody another beer and slid a paycheck across the counter. "Solid set tonight."

Kody thought about the mistakes he'd made. "Thanks."

The bartender went back into the kitchen, and the girl, after a sip of her vodka soda, turned to face Kody. "Okay. So what's your *real* job, though?"

He patted the top of his guitar bag.

The girl's tattooed leg, slung across the other, swiveled side to side like a tempting pendulum.

"Sooo, you're famous?" She swirled ice cubes with her straw.

"No. Just play as many gigs as I can and stay a few months ahead of myself with bookings." Kody noticed the girl's inconspicuous nose piercing, which glittered as she formed her next question. While she settled on one, he added, "I'm on my way down to Texas. Spending some time in Austin before heading to Nashville."

The girl's eyes twinkled. "Oh! I *love* Nashville." She clapped her hands. "My friend moved there last year, and I visited in October. We had a ton of fun."

Kody tapped a finger on the bar.

"Are you just playing there or …?"

Recognizing that the girl didn't intend on finishing the question, Kody answered, "Yeah," lifting his beer. "Doing some recording too." He braced for the interrogation.

"Recording?" she replied. "Like *your* songs?"

He nodded, taking a sip.

Swirling the ice again. "At a studio?"

"Yup."

"So, you're working with some big record producer."

Kody stared blankly at her.

"What?"

He downplayed the situation. "The guy I'm working with has some respectable credits."

The girl scooted her stool closer. "Like what?"

He tilted his glass toward her. "You know who Cal Walker is?"

"Shut up." The girl dubiously scanned Kody's face before saying, "Yes!"

Kody took a sip. "He did Cal's last album."

The girl's mouth hung open. "No way."

He nodded.

"That's *so* neat!" She slapped her thigh. "Are you super excited?"

Kody shrugged. "I'm interested to see what happens."

The girl glanced at the floor before looking at Kody. "When do you start?"

"Nine days."

Two jukebox songs passed before the girl spoke again.

Kody attempted to listen, but the previous night's lack of sleep had begun to make his head feel heavy. Some primal part of him found the idea of sleeping unacceptable and urged him to continue the conversation.

Focus! It commanded, like a determined general.

The girl kept talking.

Nod like you're listening.

Kody nodded, but he was becoming increasingly disinterested in anything that wasn't soft and stuffed with feathers. As he fantasized about falling backward into a giant down pillow, he noticed the girl looking at him expectantly. "Oh." She had asked him something. "What?"

The girl leaned forward and lowered her voice. "I asked if you're happy, doing what you do?"

3

A knock on the window startled Kody awake, and he turned beneath his blanket, which smelled like it needed a trip to the laundromat. While he waited for his morning erection to subside, there was a harder and more insistent knock, followed by a booming voice. "Anyone in there?"

"Goddammit." Kody felt this a fitting response, considering he was parked in the lot of Boise Baptist Church. He tucked what was left of his excitement between his stomach and the elastic band of his underwear. With his T-shirt covering the evidence, he flipped onto his side and slid back the curtain, flooding the inside of the van with harsh sunlight. The opening sliding door revealed a pastor, eyes wide with amusement, who quickly composed himself.

"Son, I don't know if you're aware"—the pastor leaned forward, inspecting the inside of the van—"but this is, indeed, an *active* church."

Kody's erection disappeared. "I'll be out of here in five minutes."

The pastor patted the top of the van. "God bless ya."

After crawling out the side door, Kody sat barefoot on the curb and lit his morning cigarette. Through wisps of white smoke, he watched the pastor enter the church and thought about how he should have tried to make something happen with the girl at the bar the night before. He chastised himself for not doing so, and promptly added her to the list of missed opportunities that he would use to torment himself.

Glancing back at the van, he remembered how it had stalled during his drive to the church. After some effort—and a few impassioned curse words—the Dodge had started back up.

"First the fuel line," he grumbled. "Now this."

With the cigarette hanging between his lips, Kody pulled his phone from the pocket of his flannel pants and checked his bank balance. A mental shuffling of numbers revealed that, if he was frugal, payment from his remaining gigs enroute to Nashville would provide the final funds needed to cover the recording session, which was now only eight days away.

"Going all in."

A smoldering inhalation ignited a firecracker chain of not-so-distant memories: his cramped Portland apartment; bumper-to-bumper traffic, cursing through a rain-streaked windshield; hefting another back-breaking box onto a head-high warehouse shelf before checking the clock for the hundredth time, anticipating the first of many post-shift beers.

Then he remembered the phone call from Red, his disbelief after hanging up and recognizing the lucky lottery ticket he'd drawn. Thinking that, maybe, there was a way out of the soul-sucking cycle—a shot at something resembling fulfillment and purpose.

Setting his phone on the curb, he took a drag, but the relief he felt was eclipsed by an image of himself standing on the side of the interstate, clenching his jaw while some lanky tow-truck driver secured the van. The heavy expense would be paid with a crippling swipe of the debit card ...

Kody flicked his cigarette across the lot.

For the sake of his sanity, he wrote the malfunction off as a fluke.

The van started fine, and Kody drove barefoot to a nearby truck stop. Once parked, he opened the back hatch and dug through his backpack, out of which he pulled a bar of soap (stored in an old sock), a bottle of shampoo, a towel, and some fresh clothes. He put shoes on, closed the tailgate, and walked into the station, where the tired-looking male clerk asked Kody how he was doing.

Kody ignored the question. "How much for a shower?"

"Ten."

Kody set his clothes on the counter and fished a twenty from his wallet. He gave the bill to the clerk, who opened the cash register and took out two fives. Blank-faced, the clerk handed Kody his change and slid a key across the counter. "Number four."

Kody unlocked number four and opened it, revealing a cramped, grimy restroom. As he removed his shirt and kicked off his shoes, his phone chimed, and he reached into his pocket to check the screen. There was an email from one of the venues he'd be playing in Austin. The subject read, *Your Performance.*

"Great," he mumbled.

Kody,

Though the El Borracho staff and I were looking forward to meeting you and hearing your music this week at the new tasting room, there's a local company that wants to rent the venue for a party on the same night you're scheduled to play.

Due to rising costs, this is an opportunity we need to take, so we've decided to cancel your performance.

Kody huffed and typed a terse reply before stuffing the phone into his jeans and sliding them to the floor. "Three hundred bucks down the drain." After removing his socks and underwear, he stepped into the shower and lifted the handicap seat against the soap-scummy wall to give himself more room. This was his first shower in two days, and, after blocking thoughts of all the truckers who'd likely masturbated onto the athlete's-foot-infested tile, he savored the warm water and the way the steam soothed his aching vocal cords. When the shower was over, he shaved at the sink. While washing the razor, he noticed a bloody Band-Aid in the soap holder.

4

Clean-clothed and smelling of cheap soap, Kody merged onto the highway toward Utah. He stepped on the gas, taking full advantage of the eighty-mile-per-hour speed limit. As the speedometer needle rose, the van sputtered, and Kody chose a random god.

"Zeus," he prayed aloud. "Get this van to Nashville."

Hands on the wheel, he leaned forward to gaze up at the monstrous clouds, illuminated through their cracks and around their edges by the golden light of heaven. Amid these clouds, Zeus was seated on a throne, and the make-believe deity laughed before hurling a massive lightning bolt that destroyed the van, Kody, and all his belongings in an instant.

An eighteen-wheeler blasted past in the oncoming lane, carrying a load of who-knows-what to Wherevertown, USA, and Kody imagined the captain at the helm of that lonesome ship. Halfway through a fourteen-hour shift, they poured peanuts from a plastic pouch into their open mouth, chewing as the punchline of some stand-up joke broke out from the speakers. The driver's laugh sent specs of snack flying onto the dash, which they wiped away with gratitude for their open-road cocoon.

The truck became a Buick, and the driver was now Father.

"I told you not to fall asleep!" he barked at young Kody, slumped in the passenger seat, who forced open his heavy eyelids. Street lamps floated past in the darkness; in his far-away mind, Kody could hear the whooshing of each one like a striking lightsaber as it rushed by.

Zooom...Zooom...Zooom.

The Buick began to drift into the oncoming lane, where a pair of distant headlights approached with steady speed. Kody glanced nervously at Father, knowing the pain that awaited if he asked the question that was congealing.

"I need my co-pilot sharp." Father lifted a can of beer from the cupholder and took a swig, easing the wheel left.

Kody's ribs constricted as he sat upright. Fearful thoughts became urgent as the headlights drew nearer. He wanted to yell, but yelling was weakness, and weakness was a punishable offense.

Take the wheel.

This decision would lead to bruises and questions from teachers, which he'd be instructed to answer with coached lines, rehearsed like multiplication tables. Oncoming doom grew brighter as the street bulbs whizzed faster.

Zooom. Zooom. Zooom. Zooom.

Kody squinted, and his fingers gripped the seat with the force of the fear that wasn't permitted to leave his trembling lips. Father pushed the pedal, which fed the growling motor, and a desperate honk erupted from the oncoming vehicle as it swerved to avoid the barrelling Buick. A throat-scraping scream burst from Kody, despite his efforts to stifle the terror that now heated his brow like an engine fire.

Shaking his head in disapproval, Father took a slow sip from the can and glanced at his young son. "Think you can stay awake now?"

The truck's specter receded in the rearview, and Kody directed his tattered attention toward that shrinking shape. Shaking his memories and the nausea they caused, he thought about how he and the unknown driver shared an intangible camaraderie—a mutual freedom to roam the highways of the nation, unchained from the monotony of some stationary and stale existence.

The Feeling surged, radiating through every nerve in Kody's body. Tears welled in his eyes, and he couldn't tell if they were good or bad. To release the mounting pressure, he roared at the windshield—at the rolling hills of Southern Idaho—emitting an inhuman sound that was both orgasmic cry and gut-wrenching dread.

Kody's voice cracked. He ran out of breath, clenched the wheel.

When the noise was done, there were no thoughts.

Only the hills, the clouds, the van, and the steady rumble of the road.

Doing **a crossword puzzle on Nashville's neon-lit Broadway** on a Friday night would require superhuman focus. To achieve this focus, one would need to block out the din of thousands of tipsy tourists, stumbling from one bar to another—yelling, laughing, and shouting questions that would yield answers not remembered the next day. In addition to the noise of people, one would also have to ignore the sound of myriad bands, which created a cacophony of crashing cymbals and blasting amplifiers that assaulted the ears from every direction.

Dane possessed superhuman focus.

The shaggy-haired blond sat on the bench seat in the back of his pedicab—legs stretched out, feet propped up on the bike seat—oblivious to the eleven o'clock madness raging around him. Breathing a mixture of exhaust fumes and humid air, Dane racked his brain for an elusive five-letter word while street hustlers sold bottled water and grocery-store-bought flowers to intoxicated passersby. Men with backpacks, leaning casually against brick facades, whispered drug names and clandestine prices into the ears of eager marks. Dolled-up prostitutes strutted the sidewalk in pairs, zeroing in on lonely businessmen who had struck out with the tourist girls and tattooed bartenders. Hot-dog vendors sold bouts of diarrhea for five dollars a pop. Cars honked. Engines revved and idled. A huge tractor rolled down the street, pulling a trailer full of sorority sisters who sang Journey's "Don't Stop Believing" at the top of their collective lungs.

"Hey, bike man!" a young voice called.

Two little Black boys, to whom Dane had given many rides, sprinted up to the pedicab. The younger one, holding a small cardboard box with candy bars inside, climbed up into the rickshaw and sat beside Dane, who smiled and closed the puzzle book.

"What's up, fellas?"

The boy on the sidewalk squeezed the bike's hand brake repeatedly and bobbed his head to the rhythm of his squeezes. Expressionless, he looked at Dane.

"Can you take us?" he asked.

Rather than answering, Dane nodded along to the hand-squeezes for several beats. Then he folded the puzzle book, slid it into his pocket, and stood in the back of the rickshaw, which wobbled under his weight. Leaning forward to grab the hand brake, Dane planted his free hand on the seat, stabilizing himself before climbing into driving position.

"All aboard, gentlemen."

The brake-squeezing boy climbed into the back of the pedicab and sat beside his friend, who counted a thick stack of cash.

Dane pumped his legs and yelled, "Comin' through!" as the bike swooped in front of a group of drunk college guys who yelled profanities while Dane pedaled across a parking lot, weaving between rows of cars.

"You boys get rich tonight?" Dane glanced over his shoulder.

The older boy replied without looking up from the stack of bills. "Mm-hmm."

The younger boy chimed in, "Someone gave us fifty dollars!"

"That's a fat tip." Dane thumbed the throttle, lightening the strain on his already sore legs. As he ascended a steep hill, fighting to steady his breath, the little candy salesmen talked about what they were going to buy with their hard-earned money.

"I'm gonna get those Rollerblades," the older one declared.

"I can buy Quicksilver Two now!" the younger boy said.

Maybe that's a video game, Dane guessed.

At the top of the hill, Dane turned onto a side street, and the older boy's phone rang. "Hey, Momma," he answered. "We're coming."

Dane felt a tap on his shoulder and looked back to see the younger kid handing him a twenty. "Pleasure doing business with you, boys." Dane tucked the cash into his pocket, and, after pulling into a gas station lot, wheeled up to the usual spot, where the older boy's mother sat in her idling car, smoking a cigarette with an elaborately manicured hand dangling out the window.

As Dane stopped the bike, the mother greeted him with honey-drizzled warmth, "Hey, shuga."

"How goes, Miss Simmons?"

The boys jumped out of the pedicab and fought over who would open the car's back door. Stiff-arming the younger one, the older boy opened it, slipped inside, and closed the door behind him. He secured the lock and cracked the window so he could taunt the younger boy, who struggled with the handle.

Miss Simmons said, "TJ, you come on up front now."

The younger boy balled his fist and glared menacingly at the older one before running around the front bumper. Miss Simmons winked at Dane, who grinned and said, "Till next time," as he whipped the bike around.

An hour after dropping off the candy boys, a redheaded bride-to-be reached out from behind Dane and grabbed his pedal-pumping thigh. Two giggling bridesmaids, one seated on either side of the bride in the back of the pedicab, filmed the groping with their phones.

"All right." Dane peeked over his shoulder with a playful smile. "The first pinch is free. After that, it's twenty dollars per squeeze."

This was the redhead's bachelorette party, and the three girls were in town from Texas. Each wore a shirt adorned with a customized Jack Daniel's logo to commemorate their Music City weekend. The bride's shirt was pink. The bridesmaids wore black.

Wobbling with the movements of the rickshaw, the bride attempted to stand, but the bridesmaids pulled her down into the seat. "If I'm gonna pay twenty for a pinch," the bride shouted. "I might as well give you a hundred for a lap dance!"

The bridesmaids snickered.

Between heaving breaths, Dane played along, "Okay. You pick three songs, and we'll make that happen when we get back to the hotel."

The girls spent the rest of the ride asking questions. Was Dane single? Was this his only job? What else did he do? Did he like cats or dogs? If he were forced to have sex with one U.S. president, which one would it be?

At twenty-eight years old, Dane *was* single, and he liked it that way. Except for playing his fiddle around town for cash, pedicabbing was his sole source of income. He was a drifter, traveling from place to place, living in his small RV, working any job that came his way, and being content to do so. Dane preferred cats over dogs because of their relaxed and low-maintenance nature. And if he were to have sex with one U.S. president, it would be Abe Lincoln.

"For starters, he's tall," Dane explained. "But that top-hat really seals the deal."

He pulled up to the valet loop at the Holiday Inn, where, once parked, he dismounted and squeezed the hand brake to stabilize the pedicab so the girls could exit safely. While stepping out, one of the bridesmaids lost her balance, toppled forward, and was caught by the bride, who laughed uncontrollably at the spectacle they'd become.

Once the girls were on the sidewalk, the bride fished a roll of sweaty cash from her jeans. "Okay, Bike Boy." She stood in front of Dane and counted three twenty-dollar bills. "Here's for the ride." As he opened his wallet, the bride stuffed five more twenties into his shorts. "And here's for my lap dance." She grinned mischievously, awaiting Dane's response.

One of the bridesmaids—a caramel-skinned beauty—whispered something to the other while looking Dane up and down.

With a smirk, he nodded and opened the rickshaw's bench seat, grabbing his cable bike lock, which he planned on using during his performance. Closing the seat, he whistled at the young valet, who was seated on a folding chair, staring at his phone. "Hey, bud."

The valet looked up.

"Ten bucks to watch the bike for a sec?"

In **the hotel room,** the bride-to-be checked her red mane in the mirror while addressing Risa, the caramel-skinned bridesmaid. "Don't tell me you're texting him again."

Risa sighed and slid the phone into her purse, which lay on the floor beside the chair where she was seated.

The bride turned to her. "You're a thousand miles away from that asshole, and you *still* can't stop thinking about him."

Sarah always had a way of making Risa feel foolish. "I just sent him a picture of that guy in the Trump costume."

"You know he's not gonna text you back."

Seated on the edge of the bed, the other bridesmaid, a bespectacled Korean American named Melanie, snapped her fingers at Risa. "Forget about Vithu." She leaned forward, pointing a thumb over her shoulder. "We're about to get a strip show from this hot bike-taxi guy."

Risa brushed a wisp of curly brown hair out of her eye and lowered her voice, not wanting Dane, who was getting ready in the bathroom, to hear. "He *is* cute." She glanced at Sarah, shaking her head. "How do you always get us into these situations?"

Sarah arched her back proudly and placed a hand on her hip, flicking her hair in a theatrical manner. "Only one life to live, babe." She plopped onto the bed beside Melanie and threw an arm over her shoulder. "And you best believe we're gonna come out of it with some stories to tell."

Risa smiled.

"Wait," Melanie said to Sarah. "We should set Ree up with Bike Boy."

Risa leaned forward, shushing her friends with a finger to her mouth.

Sarah's eyebrows jumped.

"Yeeeah," Melanie continued with an impish grin, pointing at Risa. "Time to get that booty-call off the brain."

"Vithu's not just a booty-call," Risa said, rubbing the side of her neck.

"Yeah?" Sarah cocked her head. "When's the last time you two went out and *did* anything together?" Inspecting her nails, she glanced sideways at Risa. "Go ahead. I'll wait."

Risa knew Sarah was right, and she looked down at her purse, wondering if he'd responded.

"Don't even think about it," Sarah commanded.

The bathroom door cracked open, and Dane called out. "Is the bride ready for her dance?"

Risa and Melanie glanced at each other in anticipation, while Sarah stood, announcing, "Been ready, babe."

"All right." A slow, grinding rap song began to play through the speaker on the bureau, and Dane reached an arm through the cracked bathroom door, flicking the lights off. "Have a seat on the edge of the bed."

The following evening, after Dane had stashed the bike at the garage and counted his spoils, he hopped into his car and headed to East Nashville to meet the bachelorette party for their last night in town. His striptease had been such a hit that the girls had insisted he join them for drinks. As he crossed the bridge over the Cumberland River, he blew a kiss to the glittering Music City skyline, grateful for the exciting opportunity the place had given him.

When Dane stepped from the bar onto the crowded dirt patio, the bridesmaids hooted and whistled from the back corner.

"Heeey, Bike Boy!"

Several folks glanced at Dane, who took a sip of whiskey before squeezing through the mob. Once at the picnic table near the rear fence, he lifted his glass. "Evening, girls."

Sarah, seated with her back to Dane, turned around to stuff a dollar into his beltline. "Whaddaya think about another dance?" she asked, flush-faced and cheerful.

"It's gonna cost more than that." Dane smirked and slid the dollar into his pocket. "Plus, I didn't bring my bike lock."

Risa squealed before reaching across the table with her purse strap and throwing it over Sarah's head. Standing, she shuffled to the side of the table and positioned herself in front of Sarah, who kept the strap around her neck. As Risa began to gyrate seductively, she used the strap to pull Sarah, laughing, into her tank-top-covered breasts. Risa wiggled back and forth, and Sarah ducked out from under the strap while playfully shoving the giggling Risa into the rickety fence behind her.

Dane took a seat beside Sarah, who ran her hands through a now-messy red mane, and Risa reclaimed her spot on the other side of the table. As she settled in, Dane said, "You've got some pretty hot moves, Risa." She brushed a hand through her brown curls. "If the whole travel-nurse thing doesn't work out, you might have a future in dancing."

Risa snapped her fingers and shuffled her shoulders.

Melanie, seated across the table from Dane, removed her glasses and wiped them with her shirt. "How many lap dances did you give tonight?" She replaced her spectacles.

"Only three," Dane played along, sipping his whiskey. "What'd you girls get into?"

Sarah turned toward Dane and touched his arm. "Have you been to Panelle's?"

"Not yet. Did you go?"

"It's the coolest place!" Melanie said. "A cute old house turned into a soul food restaurant. We went for brunch, and they sat us at a big wooden table with fifteen strangers. We passed around meat and grits and collard greens and corn on the cob." She gestured with both hands. "A *ridiculous* amount of food."

Risa touched a palm to the table in front of Dane. "It was amazing." Her coffee-colored eyes shone brightly. "I ate, like, ten of everything."

"You know what they need there?" Sarah scanned her audience. "Beds! So you can nap after you stuff your face."

As the girls laughed and talked, Dane soaked in the scene. Normally, the tourists attracted to Nashville's bachelorette scene were a bore, so he felt fortunate to be in the company of three fun and spirited women. In particular, he was stricken by Risa, who radiated a contagious vitality. She was present and engaging, fully immersed in each interaction. Gazing at her, Dane took a slow sip.

Risa, listening to Sarah, glanced sideways at Dane, and a knowing smile pulled at the corners of her lips.

"Besides the pecan pie," Sarah continued, "the no-phone thing was probably my favorite part of the whole experience."

"I loved that," Melanie said, leaning in. "I wish more places would do it."

"What's the no-phone thing?" Dane asked.

Risa held an open palm toward him. "Give me your phone."

Dane scanned the girls with pseudo-suspicion. "Oh, I get it. This alleged hang was just a set-up for a robbery." No one laughed, and he moved on. "All right." He dug into his pocket and handed the phone to Risa. "You win."

She tucked the phone under her leg, and said, "There," with a wry grin.

Dane tilted his head.

Sarah explained, "At Panelle's, you're not allowed to use your phone at the table, which is so nice because then you're *forced* to interact with one another." She rubbed her stomach. "By the end of the meal, everyone there felt like one big fat family."

"Except for that creepy guy from Florida," Melanie added.

"Naturally."

"That's a cool concept," Dane said. "How do they enforce it though?"

Melanie answered, "For each text they catch you sending." She made a chopping motion with her hand. "They take off one of your fingers."

Sarah giggled and sipped at her straw.

"Who's Sutton?" Risa asked, scrolling through Dane's phone.

Shaking his head with an amused smile, Dane leaned across the table to snatch the phone from her. "Buddy of mine who's playing in Printer's Alley tonight." He glanced at the screen. "Looks like he's starting up in about an hour, so I'm planning on heading that way."

"What kind of music does he do?" Risa asked.

"Blues." Dane slid the phone into his pocket. "Great guitar player."

Risa looked at the girls. "We *have* to go."

"No way, Ree," Melanie said. "My brain still hurts from last night." She shook her head. "I'm done after this."

Sarah nodded. "Me too, babe. I'm dead."

"Oh, come *on*," Risa urged. "*You*, Sarah? Miss I'm-not-gonna-get-any-sleep-in-Nashville?"

While looking at Risa, Sarah slapped Dane across the back. "Have Bike Boy take you." She cupped a hand around her mouth, whispering loud enough for all to hear. "You've got your pepper spray, right?" Sarah squeezed Dane's arm. "Even if you don't, he's a skinny one. You could probably take him."

Melanie nodded. "Definitely."

Sarah turned to Dane. "*Seriously*, though." She leaned closer. "If I hear that you treated Ree like anything less than the goddess she is"—she pointed a sharp fingernail at Melanie—"Mel and I are going to come back to Nashville and find you."

Dane's insides churned with excitement as he imagined his alone time with Risa. Tempering his reaction, he flashed a cool grin, and said, "Promise?"

9

Mid-song, someone clapped loudly, and Kody opened his eyes, thinking the applause may have been for him. This short-lived hope was shot dead when Kody realized the man was cheering for the Utah Jazz, who were closing in on the Knicks from behind.

The applauding basketball fan, along with several other patrons of the dingy Salt Lake City pub, faced a ceiling-mounted television in the corner, leaving Kody to play music to their backs. After the song was finished, a man, roughly fifty years old, stood and walked toward the stage, raising a hand as he approached.

Kody leaned forward.

"What time will you finish?" the man asked.

Kody's already bruised ego deflated further. "Three more songs."

"Good." The man scrutinized the open suitcase that Kody used to display his merchandise. "Can't watch a game with no damn sound." He shuffled back to his stool.

As Kody began the next song, he reminded himself of the paycheck he would receive at the end of the night. He also noticed an obese white woman seated alone at a table near the window. While Kody strummed his guitar, the woman watched fixedly and tapped her finger to the beat. The intensity of her focus caused Kody to fumble a chord change, but he recovered swiftly, reminding himself that the point of playing music was for people to listen. Closing his eyes, he let go, allowing himself to become lost in the sounds, his whole consciousness being woven into a tapestry of notes. When this happened—total immersion in song—Kody achieved a state of relative peace that eclipsed any sensation he'd experienced. After entering that state nearly every night for nine months straight, he'd become an addict.

His ability to disappear into that auditory asylum, along with the lone applause of the woman, carried Kody through to the end of the set. When he muted his guitar and stooped to unplug the cable, she shuffled toward the stage and inspected the CDs in the suitcase. "Do you sell many of these?"

Kody wrapped the cable. "No. But I still put them out."

"Well, I'm pretty sure I still have a CD player somewhere." She dropped a ten into Kody's tip jar. "Will you sign one for me?"

Kody hated this question, thinking it was stupid to ask someone playing in a grungy pub for their autograph. He deployed his standard excuse, "I don't have a pen."

"Hold on." The woman headed toward her table.

The sound of thousands of cheering sports fans filled the room, and a gruff voice from the bar yelled, "That's right, boys!"

Closing his eyes, Kody listened to the TV and imagined strutting onto some massive stage, hearing the glorious roar of the crowd, feeling all that noise being made for him.

"Here you go."

Kody opened his eyes. In the woman's hands were the CD booklet and a pen, which he took to a nearby table. The bartender watched with silent judgment. On the booklet, Kody scrawled, *Thanks for the support.* Below this, he scribbled an indecipherable signature.

"You're really good, you know." The woman stood close.

Taking a step back, Kody handed her the CD and said, "Thanks," because he knew that's what people should say when complimented.

On the other side of the room, a man slammed his fist on the bar and yelled, "Come on, you bastard!"

A memory hijacked Kody's vision: Father's plum-colored face, contorted with rage as he punched a hole in the living room wall. Hot tears streaked down young Kody's cheeks as red and blue lights flashed outside.

"Could I?" The woman glanced at the pen in Kody's hand.

"Oh." He gave it back to her.

After a short silence, she said, "Thanks," and left Kody alone.

"This place is **perfect.**" Risa's knee brushed against Dane's as she craned her neck to peek over the railing. On the floor below the balcony where she and Dane were seated, several circular tables were arranged in front of a stage where a band, fronted by Dane's friend, played their Nashville brand of blues.

"You two good?" the server asked.

Dane looked at Risa, who nodded.

"I'll have another." Dane pointed to his empty glass.

The server headed toward the balcony bar.

"So," Dane spoke over the band's muddy rhythm, "a few years back, when they were renovating the building next to this one"—Risa leaned closer—"some workers found an underground tunnel that led all the way from this alley down to the river. They compared the tunnel with some others, found in other cities, and those had been dated back to Prohibition." Risa glanced at Dane's stubble-surrounded lips before focusing on his clear blue eyes. "After some research, the powers that be decided that this tunnel, here, was constructed by famous mafia dude, Al Capone, who'd come down the river from Chicago to traffic booze up to this alley, where he could sell it to the public."

Risa didn't care about Al Capone, or this story, but she liked that Dane wanted to tell it to her. She tilted her head and said, "Really?" to make Dane feel like she was interested.

"Pretty cool, right?" Dane asked.

"So cool."

The band struck the last note of the song and silenced their instruments. When the audience realized what had happened, conversations hushed, and the room erupted with applause.

Dane's buddy, Sutton, a tall, handsome white man with a cowboy hat, spoke into the microphone. "Thank, you ladies, gentlemen, and everyone in between." He pointed a thumb over his shoulder. "The band and I are gonna take a quick breather." Sutton removed his cowboy hat and wiped the sweat from his forehead with a handkerchief. "If you're enjoying yourselves half as much as it sounds like you are, go ahead and drop some appreciation in there for us." He pointed toward a spittoon sitting on a barstool in front of the stage. "It's not that we need the money." He returned the hat to his head. "It's the people we owe money *to*."

The drummer and keyboardist grabbed their drinks and stood while the other players rested their instruments on stands.

"They're great," Risa said, particularly impressed by Sutton's virtuosic guitar work. "How do you know him?"

The server set a whiskey on the table, and Dane rubbed a palm across his jawline. "I was playing on Broadway one night, and he walked by with his guitar and asked to join me for a few songs."

"Playing?" Risa asked. "Playing what?"

Dane mimed the sawing of a violin bow. "Fiddle."

"Oh, right! I used to play an instrument too, you know."

Dane's eyes narrowed. "Yeah? What'd you play?"

"Triangle." She smirked, leaning closer. "And I was sooo good too!"

"You know," Dane replied. "People joke about the triangle, but have you ever heard someone really *play* one? That little thing can really tie a band together."

"Who says I'm joking?"

Dane pointed a thumb back at himself.

"Okay." Risa shifted in her seat, peering through the balusters. "Maybe that drummer has one I could borrow ..."

Her attention was drawn back to their table as a broad hand rested on Dane's shoulder, and a smooth southern voice said, "Glad you could make it out, brother."

Risa stood. "You were wonderful!"

Sutton tipped the brim of his hat. "Thank ya, darlin.'"

Dane stood up and gave Sutton a hug—the kind men often give, with several pats on the back in lieu of a continued embrace.

As they separated, Dane said, "Band sounds tight, man."

Sutton gestured toward the stage. "The boys are pros."

Risa introduced herself and presented a hand.

Sutton shook it, said his name, and shot Dane a glance that seemed to say, *Nicely done, sir.*

"Y'all wanna hear something wild?" Sutton leaned in. "That bassist just wrapped a tour with Cal Walker."

Risa gasped and dropped her voice an octave, singing in an exaggerated country twang. *"I wonder how it'd feel to be your man."* She made herself laugh.

Dane asked Sutton, "How'd you line *that* up?"

"A lot of these downtown cats, this is how they pay the rent when they aren't on the road. I met Gene through a friend of a friend. He was looking for work outside the pop-country world, and the blues band was a good fit."

Someone yelled from the bar, "Ay, Sutton!" It was the other guitarist, waving him over.

Sutton placed a hand on Dane's shoulder. "'Scuse me. Gotta head over there."

He looked at Risa. "Lady downstairs offered us a hundred bucks to play this B. B. King tune, so Rob and I are gonna spitball some solo ideas real quick."

"Before you go." Risa fished a ticket stub from her purse and held it toward Sutton. "Would you mind signing this?" She smiled. "I'm gonna sell it when you hit the big time."

Sutton pulled a marker from his breast pocket and took the ticket stub, which he autographed. "Here you go, darlin'." He handed the stub back to her and pointed at Dane. "You're lucky to meet this guy. He's a solid one." Sutton looked at Dane. "And you ..." He glanced at Risa before focusing again on his friend. "You already know how lucky *you* are." Sutton nodded. "'Preciate you both comin' out."

As Sutton strutted across the room, Risa and Dane took their seats. He rested an arm on the circular table, facing her, and she sat with one leg over the other, facing him. Dane's warm blue eyes fixed on her, and she found herself unable to look away. Those eyes seemed to know her—perceiving subtleties of her psyche safely tucked away. Tension buzzed in the silence between them as Risa searched for something to say, a way to—

"I love looking at you."

Caught off guard, Risa felt herself flush. "Yeah?"

Dane nodded. "It's something about the way your mind works, how you engage with the world." A thoughtful pause. "You just seem so plugged in." He lifted his glass. "And the fact that you're gorgeous doesn't hurt either." He took a sip of whiskey. "What's your ethnicity?"

Risa gave him ten points for not asking "What are you?" and answered, "Puerto Rican."

Dane made an *mmm* sound, as if he were savoring something delicious. "I would've guessed Swedish."

Risa stifled a laugh and shook her head. "Such a dumb joke."

He smiled. "Yeah. About half of mine suck." He set his glass on the table and leaned forward, resting his elbows on his knees. "What time do you fly out tomorrow?"

"Early."

He glanced at the carpet before looking back at Risa. "How early?"

Slowly, she leaned forward in the same fashion as him. Their faces were close. "Seven."

"Oooof." Dane shook his head as if her answer pained him. "Why?"

Risa began to bite her lip but stopped herself. "Cheaper flight."

The room's intoxicated chatter seemed to fade as, with a single nod of his head, Dane said resolutely, "I wanna kiss you."

Risa snickered, and her heart hastened. She looked left, then right, surveying the other tables. No one was watching. Out of her peripheral, she noticed Dane's finger tracing circles on his thigh. *Why not?* Looking into his eyes, she flashed a seductive smirk. "I'll allow it."

Dane grinned and lifted a finger beneath Risa's chin, pulling her in as she rested her hands on his knees. Their lips touched, and an exhilarating spark shot through her. The sensation intensified as Dane slid his hand back, just below Risa's ear, bringing her closer.

"Okay, kids!" The server was standing over them. "No more of that."

Risa rubbed the back of her hand across her lips and giggled, unwilling to make eye contact with the server. Dane dipped his head with a playful smile and waved apologetically.

"You're gonna get us kicked out!" Risa punched Dane's knee.

Dane scratched the back of his shaggy head. "For that." He pointed a finger back and forth between them. "I'm willing to risk it."

Down on the stage, with a click of the drumsticks, the band jumped into a bluesy number, and Risa and Dane scooted their chairs together to watch. After a minute spent slowing her breathing, Risa leaned in. "Do you ever come down to Austin?"

Dane stretched an arm across the back of Risa's chair and spoke into her ear. "Haven't been in a while, but I'd definitely go back." He paused. "How long are you at that hospital down there?"

"Two more months."

Dane leaned back. "Then what?"

Risa shrugged. "I haven't decided yet, but I'm leaning toward California. Maybe San Diego or Santa Cruz."

"For real?" Dane pointed at himself. "I'm from Half Moon Bay, just up the road from Santa Cruz." He took a sip of whiskey. "Ever been out that way?"

"You look like a beach boy." Risa tugged on a tuft of Dane's blond hair. "No, I haven't, but I've always wanted to see the West Coast. I think it'd be so fun to live out there for a summer, have bonfires on the sand. I'd *love* to try surfing."

Dane shook his head. "You've got a pretty exciting life. Traveling to new places for a few months at a time, healing the sick—"

"Changing their bedpans, sticking needles in their arms," Risa added. "Actually ..." She grabbed Dane's forearm. "You've got some *good* veins." Risa bent forward to get a better look. "Oh yeeeah." She poked at a bulging one. "This guy here." She looked up at Dane. "Okay, I know it sounds weird, but there's something so satisfying about getting an IV to go in on the first try." She pressed a finger into his skin. "When it just *slides* right in."

Dane chuckled and wiggled his arm free. "All right, creep."

The keyboard player began a fiery solo, and her fingers danced across the keys in a blur of impassioned expression. After smashing out a series of chords, she held a gritty, high-pitched note while stiffening her arms and raising herself off the seat as though the keys were delivering an electric shock.

Watching this spectacle, Risa rested the back of her head against Dane's arm and wished she didn't have to leave in the morning. *He's fun,* she thought. *I wonder if he'll try to kiss me again.*

Dane squeezed Risa's shoulder. "Hey."

She glanced at him.

"Wanna take a walk by the river?"

Risa leaned forward and reached into her purse, pulling out her phone. When the screen lit up, she made a sucking noise through pursed lips, assessing whether more time with the bike boy would be worth an exhausted morning. She pictured her flight home, then she thought of Vithu. Being out with another guy made her feel guilty, but Sarah's voice popped into her head.

That douchewad still *hasn't texted you back!*

After sliding the phone into her bag, Risa released a surrendering breath and looked at Dane.

"I guess I can sleep on the plane."

Kody smelled gasoline on the outskirts of Albuquerque.
Scanning the highway, he didn't see any oil rigs that may have been responsible for the stink, so he pulled the van onto the shoulder. After waiting for an RV to rush past, he opened the door and stepped onto the asphalt. The petroleum odor was potent as he circled around to the passenger side, where he dropped to push-up position and peered beneath the van.

A steady stream of fuel gushed onto the blacktop.

Kody's anger tightened like a vise around his temples. With a growl, he pushed himself upright, and, standing beside the bleeding vehicle, did what he had been told to do in stressful situations: breathe deeply, remain calm.

His bank balance appeared in his racing mind, and the fear began to creep in, along with towing fees and repair bills.

He remembered the phone call with his mother before he'd hit the road.

"You really should get a credit card, Kody." She moved the phone away from her mouth to clear phlegm from her throat. After a drag of her spliff, she added, "I hate the idea of you running around out there with no safety net."

His tarnished credit had allowed him access to only the least desirable of card companies, and years of unfortunate circumstances had pushed those cards to their limits. Rather than tell his mother about this strangling financial noose, he'd simply replied, "If I need more money, I'll make more money."

Furious at his situation, Kody marched around the front bumper as a sedan blew by. He opened the door and thrust himself inside. After lowering the windows to dissipate the headache-inducing fumes, Kody searched for *mechanics near me* on his phone and saw that there was a shop off the next exit. Fishing the keys from his pocket, Kody glanced toward the Sandia Mountains, which, in the light of the setting sun, blushed pink beneath cotton-candy clouds. Thinking this would be a suitable final sight if the van exploded, Kody slid the key into the ignition, closed his eyes, and winced as he started the engine.

To his surprise, the vehicle didn't blow up.

If Kody had believed in a benevolent god, he would've thanked them.

He shifted into gear and crept along the shoulder with the hazard lights on, sticking his head out the window to avoid breathing the fumes. After a mile spent hoping no one flicked a lit cigarette his way, he pulled into the mechanic's lot, which was packed with vehicles. The shop was closed, but Kody decided he'd spend the night and talk to the mechanic in the morning. Considering the possibility of a sizable repair bill, paying for a motel room was out of the question, as was drinking away the evening's sorrows.

Leaving the windows down, Kody opened the door, climbed out, and circled around to the back, where he lifted the hatch. As he grabbed a camping chair and the guitar from beside the bed frame, a funnel cloud of fear bore down on his brain and raged across the cortex, sucking up neurons, leaving synapses disabled like weather-wrecked power lines. He unfolded the chair, plopped down in it, and—in an attempt to counteract the chaos—focused on strumming his instrument while the salmon-colored sky faded to an inky black.

Once he'd played some familiar tunes—and the mental tornado had dwindled to its usual intermittent gusts—Kody decided to work on a song he'd been tinkering with for the last month. Its title was "Sixteen Voices," and he was still unsure what the song was about. The lyrics, which had come to him in a manic burst at the end of a drunken weeknight, were laden with dark imagery— him crawling on hands and knees through the mud beneath the moon; a woman screaming from the other side of an apartment wall, her cries drowned out by the incessant chatter of swirling voices. Settling further into his camping chair, Kody experimented with new notes, rearranged some words, plugged in various chords and toiled over their order. After a while, he became stuck, feeling like a string-picking hamster on a wheel, so he stood up, folded the chair, and put it in the van along with the guitar.

He started walking.

Most of the businesses lining the run-down street were closed. Worn steel bars protected the dirty windows of a pawn shop, a convenience store, a tavern. Kody stopped beneath the glowing neon sign. In the bar, people shouted over Tejano music.

There may be girls.

Before the temptation took over, he moved along.

Two blocks ahead, the fluorescent lights of a 1950s-themed diner beckoned. Kody went in and ordered a chocolate milkshake from the high-school-age boy behind the counter. The kid, greasy-haired and pimpled, slouched as if he were ashamed to exist, afraid to make eye contact. While Kody waited for his shake, the boy wiped the steel counter with a threadbare towel, and an older male coworker, carrying a tray of burgers and fries, said, "Look out, *cabrón*!" to the boy as he hurried past. The boy pressed himself against the counter while continuing to clean with his head down, hair hanging over his eyes. The coworker chuckled to himself.

Sipping his milkshake, Kody passed the tavern on his way back to the van. Two old men were smoking outside, and one said, "Just doesn't make any goddamn sense," as the other shook his head, making a guttural noise in agreement. Kody wondered what they were talking about. Then he wanted a cigarette.

When Kody arrived at the van, he lit one up and sucked the smoke into his chest. Gazing at the sky, he thought about the boy from the diner and exhaled a cloud that dissipated into the uncaring night. Taking another tonsil-searing drag, he remembered the kids in middle school who had laughed at him, called him a faggot for wearing his jeans too tight. He threw the cigarette onto the pavement and smothered it to death with a swivel of his shoe.

Behind the mechanic's shop was a patch of dirt littered with discarded auto parts. After kicking an old muffler out of the way, Kody pitched a tent—his alternative to sleeping in the fume-filled van. To combat the chill of the desert night, he pulled some winter clothes from the vehicle, crawled into the tent, and put them on. Once he'd emerged from the flap, he stood and brushed his teeth while a dog barked in the distance. The bark turned into a whine as Kody spit onto the dirt beside some lug nuts. Shaking the toothbrush dry, he ducked through the flap, slid into the sleeping bag, and rolled onto his side.

In the blackness behind his closed eyelids, Kody saw the boy from the diner standing at the dishwasher. The boy sprayed a metallic bowl clean as his coworker snuck up from behind and pulled a small needle from his pocket. With the swiftness of a striking cobra, he pricked the boy's shoulder.

"Hey!" The boy turned to confront his cackling assailant.

The boy's face had become Kody's.

A gust of wind blew the sides of the tent as Kody opened his eyes and rolled onto his other side. His pulse thumped against the pillow, and he wished he'd bought some beer to help him sleep. As he drew a long, concentrated breath, attempting to clear his mind, a memory took hold: nine-year-old Kody banging on the inside of the locked door to the hallway closet, begging to be let out as Father laughed from the other side.

"You gonna write it?" Father's muffled voice growled.

Young Kody sniffled through sobs. "Okay."

The door flung open, and Father stood in the hallway, wearing only briefs and a collared T-shirt hugging his pudgy midsection. He handed Kody a tube of lipstick. "Good boy."

Van Morrison blared over the living room speakers as Kody followed Father through the darkness to his parents' bedroom, where Father turned the lights on and pointed at the white wall above the king-size bed. "There."

Kody wiped his wet eyes with the shoulder of his nightshirt. "What words?"

Father took a swig from a half-empty vodka bottle and looked down at the boy. "Fat. Cow."

Kody felt the tears welling up again, and Father sighed forcibly. "All right." He grabbed Kody's arm and jerked it, entering the hallway, headed back toward the closet.

"Wait!" Kody screamed.

Father released Kody's arm and pushed him toward the bed. "Write it."

Kody stumbled backward, the edge of the mattress breaking his fall. He squatted to pick up the lipstick.

"Didn't get that shitty coordination from me." Father tilted the bottle against his lips and gestured for Kody to hurry up, looking at his watch. He swallowed and wiped his mouth. "Let's go. She's home soon."

Kody wobbled as he balanced atop the mattress, making his way toward the wall. As he removed the cap from the tube of red lipstick, he heard his mother's car pulling into the driveway.

When the flashlight outside Kody's tent woke him, his drowsy mind was camping in the woods of the Pacific Northwest. He heard his brother's footsteps crunching across the dirt.

Only three miles to the lake.

Relentlessly, reality returned, and he remembered New Mexico, the gas leak, and the mechanic whom he hoped could fix it. Adrenaline surged as he stuck his hand beneath the pillow, searching for the knife he'd hidden.

A female voice commanded, "APD. Come out of the tent."

Leaving the blade, Kody unzipped the flap.

"Slowly," the officer ordered.

The flashlight shone in Kody's eyes as he stood and presented his palms.

"What are you doing here?" the officer asked as a male cop came around the building.

Kody cleared his throat. "The white van out front is mine." His voice trembled. He tried to steady it. "I had a fuel leak, so I pulled in for the night. Didn't want to sleep in the van because of the fumes."

The second officer scanned the dirt with his flashlight.

"Well, you can't sleep here," the female officer said.

"What should I do then?"

"We've notified the owner. He's on his way down." Using the light, she indicated the tent. "Pack it up."

Kody was carrying his burrito-rolled tent to the van when a pickup truck pulled into the lot and parked. A scruffy man in his fifties stepped out, greeted the officers, and walked toward Kody. "You my night security?" His arms dangled like an orangutan's.

"Got a fuel leak," Kody said.

The man swayed past Kody and dropped to the ground, sticking his head beneath the van. "Does it start?"

"Did last time."

The mechanic stood, dusted off his palms, and nodded toward the garage. "Pull it in."

The police left, and Kody parked the van in the oil-stained garage, where he sat on a stool against a wall of hanging tools. The mechanic raised the vehicle with a flimsy jack and set a red plastic creeper on the ground. Flashlight in mouth, he lay on the creeper and scooted beneath the chassis.

Kody watched nervously as the man moved around beneath the van, his feet coming dangerously close to kicking the jack loose. After a few minutes, the mechanic emerged and walked to the back of the shop where he ruffled through a box of parts.

With a fuel line in hand, the mechanic swayed like an ape toward Kody, who stood. "So this here ..." The mechanic showed Kody part of the line. "This came unfastened. But I gotcha fixed up." He pinched the end of the line. "And tell ya what." The mechanic looked Kody in the eye. "Only reason you were able to get here is 'cause *this* was being held in place by the fuel pressure." He searched Kody's face for a reaction. "If it had blown away, you'da been stuck on the interstate."

Kody was relieved that the repair was minor, but rather than voice his appreciation, he asked the question that dominated his mind. "How much?"

The mechanic rubbed a grimy palm across his sandpaper jaw. "Three hundred."

Kody pulled the phone from his pocket, studied it, and held it up for the guy to see. "For eight minutes of work?"

"Look, buddy," the mechanic said. "I didn't have to drag my ass off the couch and come down here." He pointed toward the open garage door. "I coulda just as easily told the law to send you packin' and charged you the same price to look at this hunk of shit in the morning."

Kody imagined a powerful earthquake, wishing for one. The garage would shake as several tall red toolboxes scooted forward, their drawers rattling open. Suddenly, one of the cables supporting a large fluorescent light fixture would snap, sending the casing swinging like a nine iron toward the mechanic's head.

"So what's it gonna be?" The mechanic raised an eyebrow.

Returning to reality, Kody inhaled intentionally and considered his situation. Austin was eleven hours away. His remaining gig there was in four days. During that time, he would need to replace the funds spent on this repair *and* make enough to cover the canceled performance to have enough money for recording.

I'll need to look for some work down there.

"There's an ATM at the station up the street," the mechanic said, gesturing toward the door. "I'll pull the jack while you grab the cash."

13

Side by side, Risa and Dane walked the brick path that lined the Cumberland River. Ahead of them, the scarlet LEDs that spanned the bridge danced as reflections on the meandering water.

"It's so quiet out here," Risa observed, scanning the scene that, hours ago, had been alive with partying people.

"Yeah. Different vibe this time of night."

Up the road, a street sweeper hissed as it washed away an evening's worth of filth.

Dane gestured toward the river. "All right, cool fact—in the late 1700s, this whole river froze over." Risa braced herself for more trivia that she wouldn't care to remember. "Which is how Nashville came to be. The first settlers strolled across the ice and made their homes right here, along the bluffs."

Risa appraised the brick buildings. "Hmmm."

Dane continued, "This town was actually called 'Nashborough' back then, but 'Borough' was a British term, and the settlers didn't want to be associated with the Brits, so they changed the name to Nashville."

Risa snickered, and Dane looked curiously at her.

"I think it's cute that you know all this random stuff," Risa said.

Dane chuckled at himself. "Yeah, I do slip into tour-guide mode sometimes, don't I?"

"Yep." Risa glanced at the sluggish river, then at Dane. "Tell me something about *you* now."

"What do you want to know?"

They stopped walking, and Risa grabbed one of Dane's hands, poking a juicy vein. "Do you like to dance?"

He smirked. "Sometimes."

Risa rubbed Dane's hand with her thumb and looked into his eyes. "Show me."

Dane pulled out his phone, cued up a slow ballad, and slid the phone into his pocket. He placed a palm above Risa's hip and took her hand before clearing his throat and straightening his posture in an exaggerated fashion.

When the lyrics began, Risa recognized the Cal Walker tune.

"I wonder how it'd feel to be your man."

"Good choice," she said, ignoring the droplet of rain that landed on her forearm.

As they swayed to the song's easy rhythm, Risa deactivated her default dance moves and noted the details of Dane's style, which she found to be quite simple.

Right, left, left. Right, left, left.

After a few steps, Dane raised his arm and spun Risa, who *ooohed* and, once facing him again, said, "California boy's got some spicy tricks."

"I did a lot of dancing in Texas."

"Did they teach you this one?" Risa released Dane's hand and let her arms dangle at her sides. Moving her shoulders in slow undulations, she leaned back into a limbo position, struggling not to lose her balance.

Dane grabbed one of Risa's lifeless arms and pulled her toward him. "Didn't see that one down there. What do you call it?"

"The Bernie." Risa sprouted a self-amused smile.

Their dance resumed as raindrops pattered on the brick. Dane spun Risa before stopping her mid-rotation and pulling her back against his chest. With his arms wrapped around her body, they rocked to the music, and Risa turned her head to the side, releasing a low-pitched, contented noise. She looked expectantly out of the corner of her eye as Dane lifted a hand to pull Risa's curls out of the way. Being a few inches taller than she was, he lowered his head to kiss her neck lightly just below the ear. Chills shot up her spine as she pressed her body into his. Rain poured steadily, and Dane kissed his way to Risa's jaw, then across her cheek. He pinched her chin and hovered his lips in front of hers, hesitating. Their mouths traded eager breaths. Unable to bear the anticipation, Risa reached back and clutched Dane's butt, pulling his growing heat against her.

The kiss was passionate, uninhibited.

Risa's curls dripped with rain as she turned to face Dane and stood on her tiptoes, grasping his shoulders, lifting herself to his lips. Dane grabbed the back of Risa's head with one hand and half of her ass with the other, bringing her closer, tighter.

The downpour intensified, soaking everything in the Tennessee night.

Dane peeled his mouth from Risa's and playfully smacked her thigh before grabbing an arm. "Come on." The bottoms of their shoes slapped in unison as they ran across the glistening brick.

K**ody felt a prick near his neck tattoo** and dispatched a hand at full speed. His palm struck the skin with a *thwap!*

"Son of a bitch."

In the darkness, the mosquito's wings whined like a tiny propeller plane zipping around inside the van. After removing the sleep mask from his eyes, Kody slid a hand beneath the pillow and pulled out his phone. The screen's glow illuminated the back of the vehicle, and he held the makeshift lantern above his stomach, listening for the buzz of tiny wings.

"Come on," he urged.

A diesel engine rumbled somewhere in the faraway night, and, for a split second, Kody saw the bug in the light of the phone and clapped, dropping the device onto his belly. Picking it up, he checked his palms, which were stained with bloody bits of leg and thorax.

After wiping his hands with a dirty T-shirt, Kody grabbed his keys, opened the sliding door, and climbed into the warm Texas night, which smelled of fertile soil and cow farts. Dew from the grass soaked his socks as he gazed up at twinkling diamond stars, strewn haphazardly across the soul-wrenching blackness. Kody stared at the sky, waiting for something to happen. When nothing did, he opened the driver's door, leaned in, and stuck his key into the ignition, raising the windows to prevent any more unwelcome visitors. He closed the door and climbed into the back of the van. Once on the mattress, he pulled the blanket over himself and calculated how much sleep he could get before waking for work.

Dane sat on the back seat of his car, wearing only boxer shorts. Risa lay on her back across the seat with her knees bent, bare feet on the upholstery, and her head in Dane's lap. Topless, she stared at the ceiling with her long maroon skirt pulled up to her hips. Rain hammered the roof as she gazed up at Dane and lifted a hand to rub the back of his head. "You've got a sexy heart rate, you know that?"

Dane brushed a finger across her cheek. "Something only a nurse could appreciate."

"Oh!" Risa erupted. "Hold on." She pressed an ear against Dane's stomach and furrowed her brows while making a gurgling noise. "Bluh-a-bluh-bluuuh."

Dane laughed, but Risa covered his mouth with her palm. "Wait." The rain sounded like a steady stream of marbles being sprinkled onto the roof. Straight-faced, Risa removed her hand. "Bluuurp-bla-bluuurp."

"What are you doing?" Dane asked with a grin.

Risa poked Dane's chest. "That's the noise your stomach is making."

Dane shook his head. "Why are you so funny?"

Risa groaned and hid her face with both hands before reaching up to pinch Dane's nose. "Why are you so sweet?"

"I eat a lot of candy."

Risa stuck her tongue out and made a gagging sound.

"Another bad joke?"

Risa nodded.

"That's what I was going for."

"Mission accomplished."

In the silence that followed—featuring slowly caressing fingers—Dane peered out the moisture-coated window and took a deep breath. Contentment surged within, and he glanced down at Risa, whose eyes were shut above a closed-mouth smile.

Her eyes flicked open. "I felt you looking."

"Can you feel this?" Dane moved his hips up and down, causing Risa's head to bob.

She dug her fingers into Dane's torso, trying to tickle him. When it didn't work, she gave up, and Dane searched her eyes, which glittered with life. He rubbed a palm across her bare stomach and fingered her belly button ring. "Shall we?"

Risa tilted her head back and fixed her gaze on something. Following her line of sight, Dane watched a drop of water slide slowly down the glass as, with a sigh, Risa sat up—running a hand through her unruly hair—and reached for her tank top.

16

Dane was silent as he pulled his car into the valet loop. Covertly, Risa scanned his face, wondering what he might be thinking. After slowing to a stop along the curb, he put the vehicle in park and looked at her. "Such a great time." He squeezed her thigh through the skirt. "I'm really glad you girls flagged me down last night."

Risa smiled, hoping this wasn't the last time she'd see Dane, but trying to be okay if it was. "I had so much fun." She glanced at his muscular forearm and considered prodding a vein. "Maybe I'll come back up here one day."

"Actually ..." Dane's eyes searched hers. "How would you feel about me maybe coming down to Austin next week?"

Risa laughed, but when Dane's lips pressed into a thin line, she said, "Wait," cocking her head. "You're serious?"

He nodded.

Risa's stomach did pirouettes. "Hmmm." She looked out the windshield, feigning contemplation while tapping a finger on her bottom lip. "That *might* work." She glanced at Dane. "How would you get down there?"

He knocked on the dashboard.

"You'd *drive*?"

"Yeah. I'd throw the car on the dolly and tow it with the RV. Make a road trip out of it."

"Will your job be okay with that?"

"I've been killing it the last few months. My boss loves me, and I can pretty much come and go as I please." Dane rubbed the back of his blond head. "Plus, I've got a bunch of money saved up, and I've been wanting to get away for a week or so." He pointed a thumb out the window. "I was thinking about heading to the Carolina coast, but you've got me curious about Austin again. It's been a while since I was down there." He paused. "I've got a buddy in town I'd love to see, too, so this would be a cool reason to pop back down and catch up with him."

Risa pictured the two of them dancing at some Texas honky-tonk, spinning between boot-clad couples. "Sounds fun." She raised a finger. "But we'll have to work around my shifts at the hospital."

A comfortable smile spread across Dane's face. "Awesome." He leaned closer and rested an elbow on the middle console. "I'll call you when I'm on my way down."

Risa reminded herself to breathe. "Perfection."

Dane slid a hand across Risa's back, and she leaned in for one last intoxicating kiss.

II

Confluence

17

On his hands and knees, Kody activated his headlamp and slid the dust mask over his nose and mouth. As he prepared to venture into the dank crawl space, one of the other workers shouted, "Ay!" and Kody looked up at the stocky Mexican man, who was on a ladder, hanging siding.

"Put your shirt in the glove." The worker gestured as though he were tucking long sleeves into his gloves. "The insulation. It's itchy."

Kody did as he was told before grabbing a long strip of fiberglass insulation, which he'd be dragging into the hole. As he ducked his head and took a steadying breath, the worker whistled, and Kody glanced upward.

"Look out for the shit-water," the man said with a grin.

Fighting the urge to rip off his coveralls, Kody reminded himself that he needed the money.

Van repair, seven hundred miles of fuel, two packs of smokes, all that gas-station food ...

During the drive from Albuquerque, Kody had stopped several times to browse Austin's online classifieds for work. Of the several jobs he had contacted, this one, described as *Construction Labor, no experience necessary,* had been the only one to respond. As Kody poked his head into the cobwebbed abyss, he knew immediately why the work had been given so eagerly to a traveling musician who barely knew a screw from a nail.

At first glance, the task seemed simple enough: crawl beneath the house, remove the old insulation hanging between the floor joists, and install new insulation in its place. Yet several factors made this job nearly unbearable. The May Texas weather had brought a muggy temperature of eighty-five; under the house, it felt like a hundred-degree sauna. The space between the plastic-covered ground and joists above was so narrow that Kody couldn't crawl on his hands and knees. Instead, he began dragging himself on his belly like a lizard, leaving his underside vulnerable to protruding rocks. After squirming a few feet into the crawl space, he realized the worker hadn't been kidding—a sewer pipe had burst, leaving a pool of septic water beneath the house. The putrid odor penetrated Kody's mask and caused him to gag.

Steeling himself against the onslaught of discomfort, Kody inched his way toward the back of the space. Upon arriving, he flipped onto his back and inspected the moldering insulation to be removed. He pulled the protective glasses over his eyes, which fogged as hot breath seeped from his mask. Despite his impaired vision, Kody pulled out a utility knife, rolled onto his stomach, and reached up to cut the twine that held the old insulation in place. Clumps of the stuff, like cotton candy made of dirt, fell from between the joists. As he swatted the remaining insulation down with his gloved hands, his glasses became so clouded that he couldn't see. He slid them up onto his forehead and began to itch where a gloved finger had grazed the skin. Someone hammered on the floor above him, and the repetitive thumping rattled his brain. He was sweating profusely. The fecal smell assaulted his nostrils.

Suppressing the urge to scream, Kody rolled onto his back, cut a length of twine, and stapled it to the joist above him. As he did, a tiny fiberglass particle fell gracefully—like a spiked snowflake—and landed directly on his eyeball.

18

Dane's phone rang as he crossed the Mississippi River out of Memphis. Marveling at the warm glow of a lavender sunset—illuminating clouds that floated carelessly above the tree-lined horizon—he was faced with a difficult decision: answer Risa's call or wait for the final light to fade and call her back after he'd listened to a playlist of his favorite songs. Considering the music was enhanced by the scene laid out beyond the RV's windshield, Dane opted for the latter, phoning well into Arkansas.

"*Guapo*," Risa answered.

"*Señorita bonita.*"

She snickered. "How's the drive?"

"When I stop for gas, I'm gonna send you a picture of this sunset I just had coming through Memphis. Pretty mind-blowing."

"I wanna see it. We have some gorgeous ones down here too."

"I remember that," Dane said. "They call Austin the 'City of the Violet Crown' 'cause of the vibrant colors you get."

"There you go with your trivia again."

He smiled. "What time are you off tomorrow?"

"Not early enough." Risa sighed. "We have this patient on the unit right now who yells for me like every six seconds. *Literally*, Dane, I'm not kidding. Every six seconds. If he's awake, he's yelling. And his room is right across from the nurse's station, so when you're sitting there and you look up, he's just staring at you the whole time."

"Can't you give him some drugs to knock him out?"

"Well, it's not really a yell. It's more like a—" Risa spoke in a gruff, monotone voice. "Hey ...." She waited a moment, drawing the word out this time. "Heeey ..." Another short pause. "Hey."

Dane grinned. "I could see how that would—"

"Heeey."

"Okay! I get it." He chuckled. "So unless you quit tomorrow, what time do you think you'll be done?"

"Seven. But I'll wanna head home to shower before going out."

"I like a woman in uniform."

"You like a woman with human excrement on her clothes?"

"Sounds hot."

"You're gross," Risa said. "Meet you at eight?"

"Works for me."

"Sweet. I'll text you the name of this fun little bar near my place."

"I'll send the sunset."

"Groovy."

A motorcycle blew past in the left lane, and Dane hung up before cranking the stereo and drumming his palms on the steering wheel.

19

Seated at a small table in the back of the long, wooden room, Kody allowed his awareness to shift from one beer-fueled conversation to another. In a desperate mental hunger, he raided words for nourishment, yet everything that drifted from their lips was stale, flavorless.

"This brewery just hasn't been the same since they partnered with Camden last summer."

Clinking mugs. Scraping silverware.

"It's so annoying. I always break out around my moon."

Nothing they talked about reflected reality as the battle he knew it to be. It felt as though he were wading eternally through some swamp, and their feather-light thoughts were wispy clouds streaming continuously overhead; mocking him, reminding him that he'd ventured too far into a tortured truth from which he could never return. He was ice. A hardened surface upon which their cotton-soft ideas had no hope of causing even the slightest observable effect.

Kody eyed the bar, taking inventory of many instruments leaning in cases against the counter. Their owners, seated on stools, sipped various varieties of liquid encouragement in preparation for this Austin open mic. Sign up here wasn't the standard time-slotted sheet. Instead, all performers had written their names on small paper shapes (Kody's had been a star) and placed them in an upside down cowboy hat to be drawn at random by the host.

Kody glanced at his phone: four minutes until the announcement. Considering the banking app, and his growing financial deficit, he set the device face-down on the table and took a long, calming drink of water. Earlier that day, when he'd emerged from the shit-sauna crawl space after only forty-five minutes, he'd told the contractor he was leaving, and the meaty man had shaken his head and slapped a twenty into Kody's sweating palm with a Texan send-off:

"Another millennial snowflake bites the dust."

Kody's anger burned hot as the degree to which he knew the man was right, and his fist clenched around the bill. He then swallowed the words he yearned to spit into the leathery face of that wrench-wielding ogre, who would surely pummel him at the slightest provocation. As he sulked toward his van, wiping dirt from his shirt, one of the workers called out, "That's it?"

Kody glanced toward the front-yard ditch where the man leaned on his shovel and grinned. "You just won me fifty bucks." His tool fell with an earthy thud as he whistled and jogged toward the back of the house. "Alex! Gringo didn't even make it a full hour."

Kody's self-loathing seethed, alive. Coiling in the depths of his guts, it hissed, baring poisonous fangs. Scanning the chattering brewery, Kody searched for a victim into whom this creature could leap. Seated in front of the stage were two girls in their mid-twenties, faces painted with clownlike eye-shadow and thick foundation.

Too easy.

The Thing twisted as Kody noticed an old man, dressed as a sailor, sipping a beer alone at a table near the soundbooth. "If you need a gimmick to make people pay attention to your music, it's guaranteed to be garbage."

The coils loosened, and Kody remembered his reason for coming to this place: selling records to audience members in an attempt to recoup some of the cash needed for the Nashville session. A split-second assessment put him at least eight hundred dollars in the hole.

He pictured a pleading call to Red.

"Why would I book you another weekend, Kody? I'm already losing money with your cancellation here." A sigh of resignation. "You've had months to prepare for this. I can't risk you breaking your word a second time."

Is there any equipment I can sell?

Maybe he could pawn his P.A. in Nashville before the recording, then do some street-performing to pay it back in time for his gigs in Kentucky?

Only got a few hundred for the sound system last time I hawked it.

At that moment, Kody hated his mother, who didn't have a penny to lend him. Why couldn't she have been like so many others he knew of? Like the parent of his warehouse coworker, who owned a home that would be passed along to her ungrateful spawn. Like countless women who'd chosen to make something of themselves—to pursue careers in finance or medicine—who hadn't settled for the life of a clothing-store clerk at the local outlet mall, counting down the minutes until her next cigarette break. Back at home in her low-rent trailer: anticipating a cup of frozen noodles that rotated slowly in a microwave groaning over game-show commercials.

The Thing writhed now, thrashing its scaly body and rasping so loudly that Kody scanned the room to see if anyone had heard. As he did so, his gaze met that of a blond, surfer-looking guy with a violin case slung over his shoulder. The scruffy musician nodded with lips lifted slightly at their edges as he pushed open the door to the men's bathroom, near Kody's table.

A guy like that learns just enough on his instrument to get the women excited.

The Thing's protest subsided as the open mic host, a bespectacled Latina, took the stage and began drawing names from the cowboy hat. "First up will be Tasha." The woman wrote the name down before drawing the next. "After that is Dane." She drew another. "Then we'll have Cuddling Bear." As the host continued, the fiddler emerged from the bathroom and tapped Kody on the shoulder.

"Hey, man."

Kody turned to look.

"I picked a bad time to take a piss. Did she call Dane?"

Kody nodded.

"Do you remember what number?"

"Two."

"Thanks." Dane slid his hands into the pockets of his shorts and listened while the host continued,

"Last, but not least, we've got Kody closing it out."

"Goddammit," Kody groaned.

"You're the headliner, man." Dane patted Kody's shoulder.

Playing last meant that there would be few people, if any, sticking around to hear Kody's music, which also meant dismal album sales. Instead of acknowledging Dane's comment, he stared fixedly at the stage.

"What kind of stuff are you playing?" Dane gestured toward Kody's shabby guitar bag.

"I'm not in the mood to talk."

After a pause, Dane said, "How 'bout now?"

Kody glared at him.

"All right." Dane's features flattened. "Have a good set."

Dane returned to his seat, and a petite girl took the stage. Kody prepared his mental scalpel and rubber gloves, ready to dissect the performance.

"Hey, y'all." The girl greeted the crowd in a mousey voice. "My name's Tasha Heart." She shifted nervously in cowboy boots, and Kody wondered if that was her real name. "This is something I'm still working on. So I might mess it up, but here goes anyways." As Tasha strummed the first chords, Kody noticed her rhythm was inconsistent. Her voice was acceptable, but the lyrics were generic and uninspired.

A waitress came to Kody's table. "You want anything to drink besides water, hun?"

Kody appraised the plump woman. Normally, he wouldn't drink until after his set, but his head had begun to hurt from all the sharp-edged thoughts careening around inside. He needed a respite from himself. "I'll take a shot of well whiskey and a lager."

"Preference on that beer?"

"No."

There was a maternal quality to the waitress, a compassion in the way she searched Kody's eyes. Afraid of what she might find, he averted his gaze and fingered something in the pocket of his long black coat.

"Coming right up," the waitress declared.

As she waddled toward the bar, Kody surveyed the room. Two men seated at a nearby table watched Tasha intently. At the table in front of the stage, Dane bobbed his head to the beat.

What do they see in her?

The waitress brought the drinks to Kody's table with a "Hey."

Kody recognized concern in her voice, and he glanced, side-eyed.

She rested a palm on his shoulder, rubbing it back and forth. "Whatever's eating you up, it'll pass."

It's all around me. All the time.

"The Lord just wanted me to tell you that." The waitress nodded self-assuredly before heading toward another table. Watching her go, Kody lifted the whiskey, which he'd planned on sipping, and drained it in one swift motion. As his glass hit the table, the crowd broke out in applause, and a rosy-cheeked Tasha smiled before taking a bow.

One guy, seated at the bar, called out, "Yeah, girl!"

The man was not shouting to show support, but rather so he could hear his own voice, so it would be heard by others. Disgusted by this, Kody shifted his focus toward the table in front of the stage, where Dane began tuning his violin. Once the instrument was ready, Dane grabbed a small electronic device from his violin case and stepped up onto the stage. He set the device on the ground, plugged two cables into it, and stuck the end of one cable into his fiddle. The host, at the soundboard, asked Dane to play, and he obliged with some soulful pulls of the bow, which immediately caught Kody's attention. Several drawn-out notes flowed smoothly into a well-controlled series of shorter ones that traveled up a scale with mounting excitement. At the crescendo, Dane dragged the bow across the strings and let a final chord ring out. *Yiiing!*

The tone's richness stirred Kody's insides, and he wondered where the surfer-punk had learned to play so skillfully.

"Good?" Dane asked into the microphone.

The crowd's enthusiastic applause was peppered with "Woos," which Kody deemed authentic.

Dane flashed a white-toothed smile and leaned into the mic. "That's my set.

Goodnight." He began to walk off the stage.

"No!" the people yelled.

Dane chuckled and resumed his center-stage position as the host called out, "You're all set!"

With a thumbs-up, Dane said, "Cool," then spoke into the mic, "Hey, everyone. My name's Dane. Traveling from Nashville." He held up the violin. "As you can see, I'm all alone up here with my fiddle." His blue eyes glimmered beneath the bright lights. "And I get stage fright when I'm playing by myself." He set the instrument and bow on the stool beside him. "So how'd you—" Dane smirked. "I mean, how'd *y'all* like to start a band?"

The audience hooted and clapped.

Kody felt a stinging in his guts.

"All right," Dane raised his hands above his head. "Here goes." Glancing down at the wooden stage, he stomped a steady rhythm. After a few beats, he looked at the crowd and said, "Like this," clapping his hands to the driving tempo. Everyone in the room, except Kody and the sailor, began to clap along.

Slap. SLap. SLAp. SLAP!

Once the collective beat was locked in, Dane snatched his violin and bow from the stool and played a catchy, Irish-sounding melody. After a few measures, synched perfectly with the audience's beat, Dane stomped on the pedal and ceased fiddling. The melody he'd recorded looped through the speakers as he leaned into the mic to say, "Awesome," with an uninhibited grin. Holding his violin between his cheek and shoulder, he clapped several times to make sure the crowd kept going. Like pouring gasoline on a dwindling fire, after a few beats, the room burned brightly again.

SLAP! SLAP! SLAP! SLAP!

Over the melody, Dane played a blazing lead line, which soared above the claps and stomps of spectators who swayed from side to side, exchanging excited glances.

From the back of the room, Kody analyzed the scene. And, though it may have been a side-effect of the whiskey, the stinging in his guts began to morph into something else. Watching the once-docile crowd enter a veritable clapping frenzy, Kody saw an opportunity.

If I can convince this guy to play with me, maybe do some street performing here in town, I'll bet we can make enough cash to get me back on track.

Dane stomped on the device and played a fiery, flowing scale that ascended rapidly toward the instrument's highest notes. Suddenly, he yanked the bow with impassioned force, cutting short the much-anticipated last note of the song as the crowd exploded with applause. A few people stood and yelled. One man whistled.

Kody slowly clapped his hands.

The old sailor stood proudly on stage, belting out "God Bless America" while holding a saluting hand to his forehead. Staring straight ahead, he focused intently on the gloriously waving red, white, and blue banner in his imagination.

The waitress sidled up to Kody's table. "Can I get you anything else, hun?"

Kody pointed at his empty beer glass. "Another of those." He indicated Dane, seated near the stage. "And I'll buy his next round too."

The waitress lit up. "He was so *good*, wasn't he?"

The stinging returned. "He was."

With a delighted smile, the waitress said, "Be right back with that beer."

The sailor's strident performance continued, and one of the made-up girls seated near the stage began to film the spectacle with her phone. The second girl hid her face with both hands, giggling uncontrollably. At the bar, one man's nose scrunched up as if the seaman's song smelled of rotting fish.

"Here ya go, honey." The waitress set the beer in front of Kody and made her way through the crowd. Once at the front of the room, the waitress said something to Dane, who hung an arm over the back of his chair and glanced at Kody.

On stage, the sailor straightened his arms at his sides and held the final note of the tune. This gratuitous display of lung capacity was ended with an abrupt stomp that jiggled the sailor's jowls. He then stood rigid, like a good soldier, and basked in the smattering of tepid applause that followed. At the table beside Kody, one guy leaned to another and whispered, "Thank God *that's* over."

The sailor addressed the crowd, "The first time I heard that song, it made me weep," while Dane removed a hooded sweatshirt from the back of his chair, grabbed his violin case, and began maneuvering between tables. As he approached, Kody prepared for the impending interaction, racking his brain for the best way to steer the situation.

I'll mention Nashville, working with Red.

Dane's greeting was apprehensive. "Hey, man." He indicated the waitress, who lifted drinks from the bar top. "She said you bought me a round?"

Kody nodded. "Yeah." He pointed toward Dane's fiddle. "You played well."

Dane searched Kody's face. "What was up with you earlier? Not wanting to talk and all?"

"I apologize." Kody took a sip. "My girlfriend of three years recently called it off, so I've been in a bad place lately."

An Oscar-worthy performance.

"Man." Dane shook his head. "I've definitely been there. Never easy." He touched the empty chair across from Kody. "You want some solo time, or is it cool if I join you?"

Kody gestured toward the seat. "Go ahead."

On stage, the sailor continued to talk, and the host tried to hurry him along. The sailor said he was a veteran, to which the host replied, "I'm aware of that." Mumbling something under his breath, the sailor saluted robotically before beginning another loud, patriotic song.

After draping the sweatshirt over the back of the chair, Dane set his violin case on the ground and took a seat as the waitress placed his whiskey on the table. Her eyes flicked back and forth between the men, as if Kody were her son and Dane his first playdate. "Let me know if you boys need anything."

With a cheerful shrug, she walked away, and Dane raised his glass to Kody. "Thanks, bud."

Kody hated when people called him "Bud." He thought it was condescending but toasted anyway. When the glasses clinked, Dane said, "Here's to the goat that rocked the boat, and started the boat a'buckin'. And here's to Adam, and here's to Eve, who started the world by fuckin'."

Furrowing his brows, Kody took a drink and laid the groundwork for his name-drop. "Nashville?"

Dane crossed his arms on the table. "Yep. Spent the last few days driving down here."

"What are you doing in Austin?"

Dane smirked. "Female."

Kody waited, knowing Dane would continue.

"She lives here, for now, but I met her up in Music City last weekend. Hot little Puerto Rican. A nurse." Dane sat back in his chair. "We had a really good time together, man. She was up there for a bachelorette party, and we had this exciting connection."

Kody studied Dane's mannerisms.

"I talked to her on the drive down yesterday, and we were supposed to meet at eight, but she had to push it back to ten. Something came up with her friend. So I figured I'd come play a few songs while I wait around for her." Dane rubbed the back of his scruffy head. "What about you? You live here in town?"

Kody tapped a finger on the table. "I don't live anywhere."

After a silent moment, Dane chuckled. "That's it? No explanation?"

Kody reluctantly elaborated. "I've been traveling the country and playing music for the last nine months. Usually, I sleep in my van. No home base."

"Fellow road dog, huh?" He pointed a thumb over his shoulder. "I live in my RV, twenty-six footer. Got it parked out in Dripping Springs for the next few days." He glanced at the whiskey in his glass. "Only been a couple years since I bought that thing, but we've been all over the country—the Midwest, Southwest, some time in Florida. It's a tank." He pointed at Kody. "I've always been curious about how people make the van thing work though."

Mentally, Kody rehearsed for this predictable portion of the social script.

"The toughest part, I think," Dane said, "would be not having a shower." He rubbed a hand across his chest. "I've gotta feel fresh every day."

Though no explicit question had been asked, Kody dispatched his usual response. "I have a membership for a nationwide chain of gyms. If the city I'm in doesn't have one, I use a truck stop or campground. Here, I found a guy who I'll pay to use his bathroom and—"

"Wait. What do you mean you *found* a guy?"

"In the classifieds. Online."

"Have you done this before?"

"Once."

Dane leaned forward. "And?"

Kody was unsure how to respond.

Dane raised his eyebrows. "What happened?"

"What do you mean 'What happened?'"

"I mean, you met a dude on the internet and showered at his place." Dane lifted his hands. "Nothing about that was weird?"

Kody shook his head.

Dane rubbed a palm along his jaw and drew back before glancing toward the stage, where a twenty-something guy positioned his banjo in front of a microphone.

Seeing that he may have been losing his potential moneymaker, Kody cast a hook. "I'm actually heading up to Nashville next weekend."

"Yeah?" Dane refocused on the conversation. "What for?"

"Recording session at Wagon Train Studios."

Dane pursed his lips and nodded. "That's a spendy spot." He scanned Kody. "How are you making that happen?"

"The producer I'm working with owns the studio. He's giving me a deal." Kody fought to restrain a smirk as he anticipated Dane's response.

Dane's eyes widened. "What?" He leaned forward. "You're working with Red *Smith*?"

Kody nodded, pleased that the bait had been taken.

"How?"

Kody conjured a scenario more appealing than the truth. "Red's brother lives in New Orleans. I was doing a gig at a bar on Frenchmen Street, and he happened to see me play. He filmed part of my show and sent the video to Red. I don't even know what the guy looked like, but, apparently, he grabbed one of my business cards and gave Red my number. I got a call from the producer the next day."

"That's wild," Dane said. "I bet that was a huge surprise."

"I thought it was a prank." Kody almost believed his own story. "Months later, it still feels unreal. But Red asked me to come up and do a few songs with him. Says he hears something in me and wants to connect me with some record-label people up there. So we'll see what happens."

Dane raised his glass. "Well, here's to you, Kody. Livin' the dream." He downed the whiskey. "Shit, if you ever need a fiddle player, I'll be your guy."

A corner of Kody's mouth crept upward.

21

The stone-faced bartender placed two unopened cans of beer on the counter along with two bottles of hot sauce. Dane glanced curiously at Risa, who grabbed a bottle, twisted the cap off, and filled the top of her can with spicy liquid.

"You drink it in one chug," the bartender instructed.

Dane poured hot sauce into the top of his can, and a little crimson lake rose to the aluminum rim. He set the bottle down, dug a fingernail beneath the submerged beer-tab, and locked eyes with Risa, who counted, "One, two, go!" as they cracked their tops, allowing sauce to rush into the drink. Lifting the cans, they tilted them back, and the spicy mixture cascaded down their throats. After several large gulps, Dane slammed the empty can onto the bar top. Seconds later, Risa followed suit, releasing a satisfied, "Aaaaah," as the bartender promptly disposed of the cans and presented Dane with the bill.

Glancing at Risa, Dane dug a hand into his pocket and said, "They don't mess around here." She shook her head, and Dane noticed the glares of two locals who had momentarily given up their stools so the couple could try the infamous "Flamethrower." Once the tab had been paid, Dane and Risa stood, thanking the locals with an unreciprocated nod as they passed. Dane opened the door, Risa walked through it, and they descended the front steps of the dilapidated house that cowered in the shadows of the slick new condos surrounding it.

"They don't like white people in there," Risa said as they crossed the silent street.

"Good thing I was with you."

"Well," she added, "they don't like *most* white people. Some locals get a pass, but mostly the gringos who go there are drunk-ass college kids who just make a mess of the place and are super disrespectful."

"I left a hefty tip. Hopefully that'll balance the scales a little."

Risa gave a pitying look. "It'll take a lot more than that."

They passed a corner market with paint peeling off the side. Faintly, music could be heard in the distance. The air was warm and thick and smelled of smoked beef. Across the street, two barefoot women strutted, carrying their heels.

"How was the open mic?" Risa pinched Dane's elbow.

"It was fun. Friendly people, great music. Also met this weird songwriter from Portland who asked me to do some street performing with him tomorrow." Dane patted Risa's butt to the rhythm of her steps. "I'm gonna take him up on it. Sounds like it could be a good time."

Risa blinked her long lashes. "How's he weird?"

"The guy doesn't talk much. Kinda standoffish. Pretty much the typical introverted-artist type."

"Is he good?"

Dane nodded. "Killer songwriter. One of his tunes made our waitress tear up."

"Seriously? What was it about?"

"That's the thing," Dane replied. "I'm not really sure, but he felt it, and that made other people feel it too."

"Well, if you play with this *weird* songwriter, and I'm not at the hospital, I'll be there."

The sound of a country band grew louder as Dane and Risa approached a battered one-story building. Several folks in cowboy hats, boots, and elaborate belt buckles were gathered outside, smoking and talking. The couple ambled up to the door, presented their IDs to the bouncer, and, once their wrists were stamped, ventured into the musty saloon, destined for the dance floor.

22

Across town, Kody entered a dark bar. A quick assessment of the room revealed two girls seated side-by-side at the counter. Kody spotted an open stool beside the blond and slithered toward the seat while shedding his long black coat. As he hung it on the hook below the bar, the blond smiled at him.

Kody tried to convey warmth through his eyes. "Hi."

The blond turned and said something to the brunette. As the girls laughed, Kody ignored a swelling insecurity and took his seat, scanning the taps.

"Hey," the blond said.

Kody looked at her.

"Are you single?"

Kody's eyes narrowed as he nodded. "Why?"

The blond motioned toward the brunette, who was talking with the guy beside her. "My sister just got dumped, and she wants to have some fun."

Kody glanced at the sister before appraising the blond and finding her more attractive. "I'm Kody." He extended a hand.

"Trisha." She shook it. "Hold on."

Trisha turned to say something to her sister, and the bearded bartender asked Kody what he wanted.

"One of those IPAs."

The bartender held a glass beneath the tap and pulled the handle. "Start a tab?"

Kody laid a ten on the counter. "No change."

As the bartender handed Kody the drink, Trisha said, "Okay!" and slapped a palm on the bar. She stood with glass in hand, and the sister said something to the guy before getting up. Trisha tapped on Kody's shoulder. "Let's go outside."

Kody grabbed his coat and readied himself for the requisite small talk.

On the fenced-in patio, Trisha introduced Kody to her sister, who shot Trisha a disapproving look that seemed to say, *Why are you trying to set me up with him?* Regardless, Kody attempted to make conversation. The sister wore a necklace with a tiny glass jar dangling from it. Inside the jar was a piece of amethyst.

"This is interesting." Kody indicated the jewelry. "Where'd it come from?"

Uncrossing her arms, the sister pointed at Trisha. "Her."

Kody turned to Trisha. "Okay. Where'd *you* get it?"

"Me and my ex went camping in Idaho this summer. I got it at a little flea market up there."

"Idaho?" Kody asked.

"Yeah." Trisha gestured toward her sister. "We're visiting from Washington."

"Small world," Kody said. "I'm from the Northwest too. Portland." He looked at the sister, who appeared unimpressed.

"That makes sense." Trisha replied.

The guy who'd been talking to Trisha's sister in the bar stepped onto the patio and stuck a cigarette in his mouth. As he lit it, the sister looked over her shoulder and said, "Hey!"

"Right after you got up," the guy said to her, "I remembered the name of that place."

They eased into another conversation, and Kody turned to Trisha. "How long are you in Austin?"

She rubbed a finger up and down her glass. "This is our last night."

While living in Portland, Kody had rarely left his apartment, preferring to toil endlessly with his guitar. But on the road, he'd discovered the excitement of conversing with women. The chase had hooked him. Akin to his musical state of mind, the game of seduction allowed no room for insecurity, brooding, or deep contemplation. Those headaches were forced from his consciousness, and here, in the moment, there could only be glances, touches, innuendo, stories, jokes, tension...

"Do you live here now?" Trisha asked, emerald eyes twinkling with possibility.

Kody shook his head. "Only for a couple days. I'm a traveling musician."

Trisha sized Kody up. "I could've guessed that." She squinted. "Heavy metal, right?"

Kody allowed an almost imperceptible grin. "You got it. The whole sweaty band packs into my van."

"Where's your van?" Maintaining eye contact, Trisha sipped through her straw.

Kody pointed a thumb over his shoulder. "Out back."

Trisha stared at Kody.

"Want me to show you?" he asked.

"Maybe in a sec." Trisha tugged at Kody's sleeve. "Let's go back inside."

They walked through the door and took two seats at the bar, facing the pool table. Kody rested his back against the counter. "So, I play music for drunks." He looked at Trisha. "How do you make your money?"

Trisha leaned in. "I dance for them."

"Ballet?"

Trisha found a picture on her phone and held the screen toward Kody. She was on stage, with one toned, high-heeled leg wrapped around a pole while the other leg was kicked out in front of her. Topless, Trisha gripped the pole, bending backward with a hand in her thick blond hair. Surprised by the voluptuous figure hidden beneath Trisha's loose-fitting sweatshirt, Kody pointed to the G-string in the picture and said, "Strange."

Trisha cocked her head.

"I'm wearing one just like that."

Trisha laughed and pushed Kody's shoulder.

He sipped his beer. "You like that job?"

Trisha shrugged. "Yeah."

"I'm not convinced."

She scrunched her mouth to the side and glanced upward. "I do." She focused on Kody. "I like the power of it."

Kody waited.

"I like that a man can only touch me on *my* terms." She nodded, agreeing with herself. "And I *especially* like werewolfing them."

"What?"

"You know," she said. "A werewolf is a man, most of the time. But when there's a full moon, he changes into an animal." Trisha scooted her stool closer. "I'm like the full moon. I do that to guys every night, make them turn into animals. They get stupid." Trisha pointed between her legs. "*This* makes you guys stupid."

Kody took a sip. "Humans *are* animals, though." He tilted his glass toward Trisha. "And, now that I think about it, your job might be one of the only places in society where it's safe to drop the act for a while. Where people can stop pretending to be holier than lions or monkeys because they wear neckties and have investment portfolios."

Trisha stared perplexedly, and Kody concluded that he'd gone too deep.

"So what's your move?" he asked. "How do you make them transform?"

Trisha jumped back in. "Most of the time, all it takes is the right look, or a little touch on the shoulder, or I just laugh at their dumb jokes or give them some cookie-cutter compliment." She rested the tips of two fingers on Kody's knee and began to walk them up his thigh. "All the boys come into the club acting so cool, and calm, and cocksure. But by the end of the night ..." She locked eyes with Kody and dragged her fingernails along his leg, returning her hand to her lap. "By the end of the night, they're begging for me." Smirking, she raised her drink and shrugged. "Besides all that, the fact that I can put myself through college is pretty nice too."

Kody finished his beer and set the glass on the bar behind him. "What's the most you've made in a night?"

"Seven hundred."

Kody took a deep breath and nodded.

"What about you?" Trisha asked.

"I need to take up stripping."

At the pool table, two bikers, wearing matching leather vests, talked trash as they neared the end of a game. The room was alive with college kids and tattooed thirtysomethings, spitting symphonies of slurred words and gesticulating emphatically to accentuate their points. Through the noise, the bottom of Trisha's drink made a slurping sound as she sucked the final drops through her straw.

Kody glanced at her. "Another?"

"Yes," Trisha replied. "But not here."

"There's a bar up the street."

She shook her head. "Can't leave my sister."

Kody weighed the options. "I have some whiskey in the van."

The cue ball made a loud cracking sound as it sent the eight careening for the corner pocket.

The country band played, and the people danced across boot-worn planks. Above the throng of denim jeans and sundresses hung a small chandelier, providing the dance floor's only light apart from a neon sign that glowed red from the wall behind the pedal-steel player. Years of spilt beer and Texas sweat had given the place a pungent odor that mingled with the scent of fresh popcorn, wafting from a self-serve machine near the dartboard.

Risa and Dane, taking a break from two-stepping, sat at a tiny table on the periphery of the action. Dane's arm rested across the back of Risa's chair, and she nodded toward one of the dancing couples. "That makes me happy."

A short Mexican man in his forties, his rough face peppered with pockmarks, was focused on the stunning young Filipina twirling before him. The bottom of her dress floated about her hips as she spun.

"He's got it all figured out," Dane said. "Just keep a steady pace and make sure the girl has a good time."

Risa wiggled Dane's ear. "Yeah? The professional dancer approves?"

Dane grinned. "I do."

The dancing man's cowboy hat was too big for his head. Beneath the brim, his gleaming eyes savored the girl, whose dainty hands gripped his as she grooved in bedazzled cowboy boots.

"Sense of humor is huge," Risa said, watching the pair. "But if you can dance, that's it. You've got me."

The dancing man appeared to be a regular at this dingy saloon. Earlier that night, when he had entered, he'd shaken hands with—and given hugs to—many other folks who'd then eagerly paired up and clambered onto the floor.

"I wonder what he does during the day, for work," Dane mused.

"Hmm." Risa studied the man.

"He looks hard," Dane concluded. "Like he's spent time doing tough labor."

Risa reached out and rubbed a thumb across Dane's palm. "Your hands are soft." She looked at him. "Like a newborn baby's."

Dane smiled. "My hand-modeling job requires zero callouses."

"What's the hardest work you've ever done?"

"Besides pedaling tipsy girls around Nashville?"

Risa nodded.

The band built anticipation of the song's final chord, which was stricken in unison and prolonged with flare, allowing couples the opportunity for exaggerated dips. After one such move, the dancing man pulled his partner upright, kissed her hand, and escorted her off the floor.

"I worked for a general contractor in Cleveland," Dane began. "I'd never done construction, and this guy was a total asshole—great at his job but really impatient. I showed up on the job site at seven in the morning on a Saturday, pretty hungover, and we were gonna be tearing panels off a foundation that had just been poured."

Risa noticed she was fidgeting with her skirt and stopped, focusing on Dane's story. *It feels so nice to be on an actual date.*

"These panels are long—like six feet each, a few feet tall—and they fit together to make a mold for the concrete. Once they're all put together, you pour the stuff. Then you strip the boards, and you have a foundation. So, I show up and the guy hands me a hammer and takes me over to the wall of panels, about fifteen feet high. He points to a little metal tag between two panels and tells me to knock the thing off. So I look at the tag for a second, trying to figure out how I should hit it, and the contractor yanks the hammer out of my hand, tired of waiting, and yells, 'Like this!' He swings the hammer up under the tab and hits a little lip that juts out on the bottom. Knocks the tab off the bolt that was holding it in place."

Dane took his arm out from behind Risa and faced her, using his hands to illustrate.

"Then the contractor hands me the hammer and just gives me this look, like, *Now, you do it.* So I go to the next tab and swing up underneath it a few times, but, with each hit, the thing just slowly scoots its way upward instead of getting knocked off."

Risa enjoyed how animated Dane had become, how he immersed himself in his story.

"So the guy gets pissed again and grabs the hammer from me and yells, in this thick Boston accent, 'Jesus Christ! Swing that fucker like you've got a pair of balls!' Then he knocks off three tabs in a row. *Boom, boom, boom!*"

Dane swung an imaginary hammer in front of him.

"At this point, I'm raging, which might have been the goal. If so, it worked! I grab the hammer from him and hit the next little tab with all my might, and the thing goes *Tink!* and flies right off the wall. Then the contractor looks at me, points at the wall of about a thousand more of these things, and says, 'Good. Now do 'em all.'"

A soft smile spread across Risa's face, and she squeezed Dane's thigh. "I like the way you told that. Even if you did spit a little when you did your impression of him."

Dane laughed. "If I spit, then the impression was dead-on. The guy had like three teeth left. Spit all over the place when he was barking orders."

"So *that* was your hardest job?" Risa teased.

"Yeah. I worked with that guy for a summer. Between not knowing anything about construction and his domineering personality, every day was tough." Dane stretched his arm across the back of Risa's chair. "But luckily, there were no catheters involved. Or ass-wiping. And I never had to give anybody mouth-to-mouth."

"I don't know." Risa leaned in. "Mouth-to-mouth sounds pretty good to me."

After a few moments of world-blocking bliss, their lips came apart, and a gruff voice said, "Es'cuse me?" They glanced up at the dancing man, who was standing with a calloused palm extended toward Risa. "You like a dance?"

Grabbing his hand, Risa said, "Of course!" and planted a kiss on Dane's cheek before following her partner onto the floor.

24

Trisha, in the passenger seat, passed the flask to Kody on the driver's side. The van idled. Warm air blew through the vents. Kody took a sip, screwed the cap, and set the flask on the floor. He turned to face Trisha, who, with elbows on the armrest, searched his face with wild eyes. They moved closer, and Kody reached out to pull her in. The kiss was lustful, reeking of need. Hands explored. Breath grew heavy and hot.

Kody reached a hand to the back of Trisha's head, tugging her ponytail, lifting her chin. As he kissed her neck, she moaned and raised the armrest, bringing her legs around the seat toward Kody, who squeezed her thigh and moved his lips from her neck to her mouth.

Tongues fought to establish dominance.

Trisha grabbed Kody's hand and pulled her elastic waistband open. She guided him between her legs. Massaging the dampness, Kody pried his lips from hers and looked into her eyes, working his fingers. Trisha bit her lip and dug her nails into Kody's leg, tilting her head back, inhaling sharply.

Her phone rang.

"Your sister?" Kody asked between breaths.

"I don't care."

They continued.

After a heated moment, Trisha said "Okay," and pulled Kody's hand from her leggings. "Do you have a condom?"

Kody nodded.

Trisha glanced at the bed on the other side of the metal cage.

After exiting through the passenger door, they opened the slider, kicked their shoes onto the gravel, and climbed into the back of the van. Kody closed the door and drew the curtain while Trisha peeled off her leggings and turned toward Kody, who undid his belt and slid out of his jeans.

The space was tight, but they made it work.

Afterward, they lay there, breathing heavily and staring at the ceiling.

Trisha's phone rang.

"Oh, god." She wiggled into her leggings and grabbed her panties, which she stuffed into the pocket of her sweatshirt. Kody pulled his jeans up as Trisha climbed outside and reached through the passenger door to grab her phone. Kody heard a faint, harsh voice from the speaker, and Trisha replied, "Geez. Calm down. I just went for a drink with that guy. I'm on my way back now." She hung up and peeked into the van through the open sliding door. "I've gotta go." She fixed her hair.

Kody rolled onto his side, supporting his head with a hand. "Okay."

After slipping her shoes on, Trisha leaned into the van and held up her phone. "What's your number? I'll text you, and you can let me know next time you're in Washington."

Kody knew how this would play out: they would exchange numbers, send a few texts, and never see each other again. But something about this post-hookup ritual made the one-time encounter more socially acceptable, so Kody gave Trisha his number.

"I had fun," she said, sliding the phone into her sweatshirt pocket.

Kody mustered a grin. "Send my regards to the Northwest."

Trisha waved goodbye with her fingers.

Kody was alone again.

25

A feathery voice tickled Dane's ear, and his lazy eyelids slid open. Dressed in powder-blue scrubs, Risa leaned over him. "Lock the door when you leave, okay?"

Dane reached out and squeezed her hip. "Sounds good." Beckoning with a finger, he lifted his head, and Risa leaned in for a kiss. Her mouth tasted like peppermint toothpaste. When they came apart, she rubbed a hand through his disheveled hair and said, "Have the sweetest dreams."

He did.

When he woke, a soft light illuminated the cracks between the slats of venetian blinds. He stretched beneath the thick comforter, which smelled like Risa—floral with a hint of female pheromone.

As Dane's brain organized itself, a tune crept into his consciousness, something elated and buoyant. In the past, Dane had ignored several such melodies, thinking, *I'll remember it later.* This procrastination had resulted in the loss of many potential songs, some of which Dane was sure would've been chart-topping hits.

Having learned his lesson, Dane leapt out of bed, humming the melody. He opened his violin case and grabbed the instrument before sitting on the edge of the mattress. First, he bowed an E chord, which fit well. After experimenting with a few other options, he replaced E with B, then consoled the rejected chord. "No hard feelings, bud." To complement the B, Dane added an A to the mix, which solidified the song's foundation. To liven things up, D and E were thrown in, bringing the progression to a satisfying conclusion.

Cycling through the chords, Dane hummed the new tune and thought about the night before, about dancing with Risa. With the help of this freshly formed memory, Dane began to replace the *hm-hmmm-hmms* with words, and, after several minutes of unintelligible syllables, he found some lyrics that fit.

"Ooooh, ain't it magic. While I'm sailing through those skies there in your eyes."

He tapped a bare foot on the hardwood floor.

"Ooooh, yes, it's magic. When everything in life just lines up right."

Dane chuckled, marveling at the creative process, thinking it was indeed magic.

"Ooooh, ain't it magic. While I'm swimming through those seas there in your eyes. Ooooh, yes, it's magic. When you find someone to love here in this life."

Thinking the word love was a bit excessive, Dane returned to the original lyrics.

"Ooooh, yes, it's magic. When everything in life just lines up right."

Nodding in approval, Dane leaned across the mattress, grabbed his phone from the nightstand, and opened the recording app. Resting the phone on his thigh, Dane bowed the series of drawn-out, flowing chords and started to sing, but he fumbled the first line. He deleted the file and hit *Record* again, this time making it through the first line but forgetting the words to the second. After four attempts, and four deleted takes, he finally played the newborn chorus without errors and saved the file for later, when he would write some verses. He turned the phone off, laid the violin on the bed, and stared at the backlit blinds, drawing a long breath and taking an inventory of all that he had to appreciate.

He was grateful for the new song, excited about what it would become. He was also thankful for his time with Risa. "Life comes in. Art comes out," he said, glancing toward a potted cactus on the windowsill. While tracing wayward spines with his eyes, Dane thought about the slim chances of Risa's bachelorette party being on the same corner as his pedicab during the Nashville-weekend madness.

When everything in life just lines up right.

Closing his eyes, he said, "Thank you, Everything," and allowed himself to become lost in the droning hum of the air conditioner.

Brrrmmmm.

After a tranquil moment, he remembered his plans to meet with Kody and realized that noon was approaching. Opening his eyes, Dane stood, locked the violin in its case, and made the bed. Then he dug fresh clothes from his backpack and sang the new tune as he headed for the shower.

26

The concrete-shattering rattle of a jackhammer startled Kody awake. Once his transient mind had oriented itself in the gravel lot behind the bar, Kody removed his sleep mask and climbed outside to smoke a cigarette. Afterward, he folded his blanket and tucked it, along with the pillows, beside the wooden bed frame. He grabbed his backpack, closed the slider, and went around to the driver's door to climb inside.

The van growled to life, and Kody fished dollar-store sunglasses from the glove compartment, sliding them over his bloodshot eyes. The thrill of conquest simmered somewhere beyond the fog of fatigue, and he tilted the rearview mirror so he could see himself, ruffling fingers through his matted brown hair, feeling like a man, feeling like he'd done his job—smelling like the lining of a ditchdigger's hat.

Kody made a call, and a genial male voice answered, "Hi, Kody."

"Stanley, can I come by for a shower?"

"Sure. I'll just be here working."

"Okay."

With the windows cracked, Kody drove the streets of south Austin. Beads of sweat squeezed through the pores on his brow, and the musty air weighed heavily in his gig-labored lungs. At a stoplight, he looked left. A line of people waited at a taco truck in the parking lot of a shabby gas station. The light turned green, and he drove a mile before pulling off the main drag. After winding down a long residential street, he parked along the curb in front of a quaint house surrounded by huge blue agaves. Kody turned the van off, grabbed his backpack, and headed to the front door.

When he knocked, Stanley called out, "Come in!"

Upon opening the door, Kody was stricken by the sour smell of unwashed socks. The sound of computer keys and mouse clicks came from the next room.

"In here," Stanley called.

Clothes were strewn about the unkempt space, along with half-finished bottles of soda and a plethora of junk-food wrappers. Crossing the stained carpet, Kody made his way to the room where Stanley sat at a large computer desk, typing in front of two giant screens.

Stanley finished whatever he was writing, spun around in his chair, and evaluated Kody with piercing olive eyes. "Well, hello." A small gold hoop dangled from Stanley's ear, and the sunlight coming through the sliding glass door reflected off his bald black head. "So nice to finally meet you."

"Hey, Stanley." Kody fished a bill from his pocket. "Here's twenty. I'll give you another ten tomorrow."

Stanley stood and accepted the payment, locking eyes with Kody. "That works just fine." He glanced at Kody's neck tattoo and cocked his head to the side. "What's that? A worm?"

Kody sighed. "It's a snake."

Stanley's forehead crinkled as he leaned closer. "Looks like a worm."

"Well, it isn't."

Stanley nodded toward the hallway. "Let me show you the shower."

They walked past the desk and maneuvered around the weight machine into the hallway.

"My bedroom is here." Stanley knocked on a door before pointing toward the end of the hall. "And that's the bathroom." He wheeled around and stood on his toes, inspecting Kody's backpack.

"You have a towel in there?"

"Yeah."

"Soap?"

"Uh-huh."

"Shampoo?"

Kody nodded.

"How 'bout conditioner?"

"No."

"Would you like some?"

"Don't use it."

Considering Stanley's lack of hair, Kody wondered why he had shampoo and conditioner. Rather than ask and prolong the interaction, he erased the question from his mind.

"Well, then." Stanley pressed his back against the wall, squeezing past Kody, inching toward the computer room. "It's all yours." He glanced at Kody's ass. "Let me know if you need anything else."

As Stanley left the hallway, Kody shuffled into the bathroom and closed the door. While locking it, he made a note to himself: *Tomorrow, bring the pepper spray.*

III

Little Boy Blue
& the Man in the Moon

27

"Sooo," Sarah said over the phone. "How's Bike Boy?"

Risa swallowed a forkful of salad. "Okay. At first I thought it was gonna be weird having him come down here. Actually, I almost canceled. Like, what if we had this really good time up in Nashville, but it was just one of those vacation flings that feels good in the moment and then turns awkward if you try to make it into something more?"

A female nurse, seated at the other end of the break-room table, nodded while looking at her phone.

"So, I'm guessing it was good then?" Sarah asked.

"*So* good," Risa replied. "It's crazy how easy it is to be with him. We just have so much fun together." She took a sip of water. "I showed him that little house-bar near my place, and then we went dancing, and we made a ton of dumb jokes, and had some serious talks too—"

"What about Vithu?"

Risa poked at a cherry tomato with her fork. "Well, we haven't had the 'we're official' conversation yet."

"Yeah, but he *isn't just a booty-call,* right?"

Risa sighed, knowing what Sarah wanted to hear. "Okay, fine. You were right. Hooking up is all we—"

"What was that?"

"I said hooking up is all—"

"No. The other part."

Risa laughed. "You were right!"

Sarah's grin was audible. "That's what I thought."

Risa continued, "Anyway, the sex with Vithu is good—"

"Good?" Sarah teased.

The other nurse glanced up from her phone.

Risa lowered her voice. "Sarah, it's great. And that's fine, but there isn't any connection beyond that." She flicked a piece of lettuce around inside the plastic container. "I'm tired of it. I'm tired of just *hanging out* with guys." She shook her head. "It seems like that's all they ever want. And I've told you, anytime I try for something deeper, they just end up getting super distant or vanishing altogether." She lifted some spinach leaves toward her mouth. "I'm looking for something else. I want something like what you and Craig have. I want to *love* someone."

"Do you think Vithu would be pissed if he found out about Bike Boy?"

Risa chewed, swallowed. "He would."

"Careful, Ree."

Risa stabbed at the cherry tomato, but the dressing had made it slippery, and the fork slid off. "Yeah. I just have to feel out the next few days. Who knows? Maybe Dane's visit is just for fun too. I don't really know what he wants. And right now, it's probably too soon to be thinking about that anyway."

"But you *are* thinking about it," Sarah replied.

Risa impaled the tomato and popped it into her mouth, speaking while chewing. "Yep." She nodded. "It's official. I like him."

"Well, tell him I want another lap dance."

Risa chuckled, trying to keep tomato mush from flying out of her mouth. "I will."

"All right, babe. I'm gonna go."

"Okay. I'll call you when I get my schedule so we can talk about the Dallas trip."

"Coolio."

"Byeee."

Risa hung up and took another bite of salad. As she chewed, a middle-aged female nurse burst into the break room and rushed toward the refrigerator. She opened the door, grabbed a bottled shake, and took a long gulp. After returning the bottle to the shelf, she closed the refrigerator and sat in the empty chair beside Risa, pulling a small mirror and lipstick from her bag.

"What are you doing?" Risa asked.

The nurse applied a coat of scarlet to her pursed lips. "A cop got shot last night, and they've got him down on the fourth floor."

"You know him?"

The nurse turned to Risa. "No." Her eyes twinkled. "But a bunch of his hot, uniformed friends are in the waiting room right now."

28

Dane meandered up to the bench and rested his violin case beside him as he sat. The Mueller farmer's market occupied the grounds of an out-of-commission airport that had been transformed into an upscale neighborhood and shopping area. Inside an open-ended hangar—spacious enough to house a small jet—several vendors had set up their booths. The road between this hangar and a sizable pond had been closed to vehicles and was now replete with tents and tables. Scores of people wandered about, casually perusing the assortment of local wares and eating tasty morsels from a variety of food trucks. Dane watched as some of these folks regarded Kody, whose eyes were shut while he strummed his guitar between a tie-dyed clothing tent and a booth selling acrylic paintings.

Wearing the long black coat, Kody crooned sorrowfully, hunching forward as though he were being tugged from the front by some invisible entity. Beside him was an open suitcase elevated by a metal stand. Inside the case were his albums, a business card holder stashed with cards, and an empty drink pitcher with a two-dollar bill taped to the brim.

The money flapped in the breeze as if it were trying to fly away.

A young female couple stopped to listen to Kody, and he opened his eyes before promptly shutting them again and returning to his song-induced trance. One of the women whispered something to the other. She nodded, and they walked away. When the song ended, there was no applause, and Kody muttered to himself before reaching into his pocket and checking his phone.

Dane stood with his violin case and moved through the crowd to greet Kody. "Hey, man."

"Didn't we say noon?" Kody returned the phone to his pocket.

"Yeah, sorry." Dane knelt and laid his case on the ground. "I slept in. Long night with Risa." He opened the case. "Had a song come to me right after I woke up too! You know, one of those melodies that just hits you out of nowhere."

"A violin part?"

"Well." Dane tuned his instrument. "I wrote it on violin, but I'll play it on guitar. Better for accompanying myself."

Kody's voice sharpened. "You sing too?"

"I guess you could call it that." Dane closed the case and stashed it beside a sandbag that was tied to the metal leg of a clothing tent. "What do you wanna play first?" He stood with his fiddle in position.

"Let's do 'Wagon Wheel.'"

Dane shot Kody an amused look. "Yeah?"

"Like it or not, it's a crowd-pleaser."

Dane shrugged. "You're the boss."

Kody counted one, two, three, and they were off.

Planting his feet in a wide stance, Dane burst into a whimsical fiddle part, swaying with the motions of his bow. His musical instincts were sharp, and the chosen notes perfectly complemented Kody's chords. A woman, pushing a stroller, slowed to a stop and held her phone at eye-level to capture the performance as her tiny boy, restrained by a seatbelt, reached his arms toward the musicians. This gesture, along with the music, acted like a magnet that attracted the attention of several passersby, who found spots to stop and watch the show.

The herd mentality taking hold, Kody thought.

Though he was relieved that the violin was drawing a crowd like he'd planned, it stung that he couldn't generate this kind of attention on his own. Shaking the thought, he sang the first verse. After a few words, an elderly man with a tennis-ball-bottomed walker shambled toward the suitcase and dropped a five into the pitcher. He waved a spotted hand at Dane, who nodded and said, "Thanks."

The man left with the speed of a tranquilized tortoise as a Hispanic family took a seat on a bench across the street. Their youngest girl, clapping in time with the music, periodically looked up at her mother and flashed a missing-toothed grin. Standing beside the bench was a hippie couple in their thirties. The man watched from behind the woman with his chin resting on her shoulder and his thumbs hooked through the belt loops of her bell-bottomed jeans.

Under the weight of this extra attention, Kody felt uncomfortably warm. As his eyes darted from one attentive face to another, he accidentally made eye contact with the hippie girl. *She knows that note was flat.* Convinced that the girl could read his mind, Kody became paranoid that she could sense how scared he was. *She hates me for being so weak.* To avoid giving his thoughts away, he closed his eyes. When he opened them again, he fixed his gaze on the ground a few feet ahead, where there was no soul to peer into his.

During the third verse, a small boy stomped awkwardly into the semicircle of open asphalt that had formed in front of the performance. Wobbling in place, the boy gazed—eyes wide with fascination—at Dane before beaming over his shoulder at his father, a red-bearded white man with glasses who stood awkwardly amongst the other onlookers. The father nodded at the boy, who turned to face the musicians and pumped his arms wildly through the space around him as though he were swatting a swarm of imaginary bees.

When the final chorus kicked in, Dane noticed several spectators mouthing the words, and he scanned their faces invitingly while beginning to sing harmony. Years of street performing had taught Dane that multiple musicians' voices made the audience feel more comfortable joining along. This was no exception. After Dane had sung the chorus' first line, several onlookers lent their voices to the mix. By the end of the chorus, a makeshift choir of united strangers was enlivening the afternoon air.

Wanting to make the most of the audience participation, Dane shot Kody a glance that suggested they prolong the song—a telepathy he'd developed after countless hours of playing with other musicians. Kody obliged, and, as the music carried on, four girls in their twenties lined up in front of the performance. The tall brunette said, "One, two, three!" and, in perfect time with one another, the girls spun around with their hands on their hips. After a few beats, they stomped and rotated the other way, shuffling several steps left. Then they stomped again, spun, and stepped to the right before clapping and repeating the dance. Many in the crowd pulled out their phones to capture the spectacle. Seeing this, Dane imagined transmissions being sent into the digital world. Thousands of miles away, folks lying on their couches and seated on toilets would watch Dane and Kody play through another chorus while the girls line-danced and the people sang along.

Once the final lyrics had passed, Dane launched into an extensive solo, using the energy of the moment to propel him toward notes and melodies that further stirred the collective exhilaration. Soon, the song's rhythm slowed, building anticipation for the closing chord, which came when Kody hammered the strings repeatedly as Dane erupted in a flurry of fantastic notes, blazing up his instrument to tones that made his own hairs stand on end. The dancing girls dispersed as the crowd cheered and applauded. In unison, Dane and Kody silenced their instruments, and the assembly's roar grew even louder.

Kody nodded abashedly, avoiding eye contact.

Dane beamed, basking in the moment.

It was customary for the lead singer to address the crowd, so Dane waited for Kody to say something to the expectant people. When Dane realized this wouldn't be happening, he took the initiative. "Thank you, everyone!" He waved a hand. "That was some great singing on your part, which means you're officially in the band now." Dane gestured toward the pitcher. "Which means we'll *all* be splitting the tips." Kody scoffed at the joke, and there were subtle chuckles from the crowd as several people reached for their wallets and lined up to drop money into the pitcher.

As the bills piled higher, the little boy took a few rubber-legged steps toward Dane, who knelt to greet the kid and looked at his father. "What's his name?"

"D-Dominic," the father replied, fidgeting with his fingers.

"All right, everybody." Dane laid his violin on the ground and reached into his back pocket. "I want you all to welcome Dominic." He produced a blue egg shaker, holding it toward the boy. "Our new percussionist!"

Dominic snatched the shaker, and Dane clapped for the kid, inspiring several spectators to follow suit. The boy squatted and placed the shaker upright on the ground. When it fell onto its side, he giggled and pushed the egg forward with a finger, watching raptly as it rolled. The father, wanting to capture this moment, dug into his pocket, searching frantically for his phone.

While he did, the moment was passing.

As the young boy played with the plastic egg, Kody eyed the half-full tip pitcher.

"Yo," Dane said, positioning the violin beneath his chin.

Kody looked at him.

"What's next?"

After a brief deliberation, Kody picked the opening lick for the Beatles' "Here Comes the Sun," and the crowd "oohed" as Dane fiddled along to the descending guitar part leading into the first verse. Mouth agape, little Dominic flailed his arms with abandon, causing the shaker, clutched between his tiny fingers, to hiss. Several women glanced lovingly at the child, purring their sentiments.

His trick is working, Kody observed.

While singing the first verse, he surveyed the crowd, contemplating the spectators' lives, wondering what had brought them to this impromptu musical moment. Glancing at the woman with the stroller, Kody suspected a recent divorce. *The husband was probably an asshole, so she got the kid.*

He inspected her ringless fingers. *Or maybe the guy died, and she's a widow.*

Finding the woman reasonably attractive, Kody fantasized about her taking a business card from his suitcase and sending him a message later that day, as the bartender in Seattle had done.

I liked your music :)

While Kody pictured this, the mother looked at him, and, when their eyes met, she scrunched her face and knelt beside the stroller to puppet her toddler's arms to the beat while singing into his ear.

"Here comes the sun. Do-doo-do-doo."

Kody's attention drifted toward the family on the bench, and, as he scanned their engaged faces, he imagined dollar signs floating above the children's heads, emblems of the rising expenses of each school year, meal, toy, and activity. The father wore a tired smile, but Kody concluded this was not an expression of his own choosing, but rather one chiseled onto his cheeks over the years by a system dependent on the molding of obedient men and women alike.

Maybe he had a few beers this morning ...

Kody was certain that, deep down, the father wanted freedom—something to hunt, an adventurous purpose to pursue—any opportunity to unleash the testosterone-fueled conqueror within. Instead, Kody watched as the man used a napkin to dab orange sherbert from his youngest daughter's face. As Kody sang the autopilot song—which he'd learned strictly for its money-making potential— he savored the renewed realization that he was the sole master of his universe, free to roam wherever he saw fit. Glancing at the man's wife, Kody relished the fact that he wasn't tied to just one woman, and memories from the previous night's encounter flashed through his mind—Trisha's nails raking the back of his head, animal passion in her eyes as she made incredible noises.

Out of his peripheral vision, Kody noticed a gray-haired man staring at him. The man's lips pursed as if he were sucking on a lemon. Suddenly, Kody realized he'd sung the same verse twice in a row.

Shit!

Closing his eyes, Kody retreated into a sanctuary of notes and rhythm, paying careful attention to his pitch and timing, making sure not to embarrass himself further. In the blackness, beyond voices singing a final chorus and the commotion of the farmer's market, Kody heard the plastic egg being shaken. The end of the tune approached, and Kody opened his eyes to look at Dane, nodding to communicate that they would finish in *one, two ...*

When *three* came, they hit the last chord, and the assembly applauded as little Dominic ran toward his father to show him the egg shaker. Taking the boy's hand, the father walked him over to Dane and pried the instrument from his fingers.

"I appreciate you doing that," the father said, presenting the shaker to Dane.

Dominic pouted and reached for the egg.

"Nah, man." Dane shook his head, pointing at the boy. "That's his now."

The father insisted on giving the shaker back, but Dane wouldn't allow it. "This is Dominic's first gig," Dane explained. "With that shaker, he'll remember this moment when he gets older." He quieted his voice and leaned in. "Plus, those are only a few bucks apiece."

After a thoughtful pause, the father acquiesced and handed the egg back to Dominic, whose face lit up again. Dane plucked a dollar from the tip pitcher and held it high, addressing the crowd. "Folks. Let's have another hand for Dominic!" The people clapped and whistled, and Dominic spun in slow circles, shaking his new toy a few inches from his face.

"Hey, little dude," Dane said.

The kid stopped spinning and stood, pigeon-toed, staring up at the fiddler.

"Since you're a part of the band now, here's your cut." Dane knelt and handed the dollar to Dominic, who stomped forth to claim his money. "That's your first dollar made playing an instrument, which officially makes you a *professional musician!*"

The father stepped forward to intercept the bill, but, when the crowd began to cheer, he relented and glanced around. He produced his wallet and approached Kody, withdrawing a twenty. "How much are those albums?" He pointed toward the suitcase.

Kody eyed the money. "That'll work."

The father shook his head. "What do you normally charge?"

Kody, the opportunist, replied, "Thirty."

"Well, tell you what." With jerky motions, the father dug into his wallet and pulled out another twenty. He dropped the bills into the tip pitcher and nodded submissively. "Keep the change."

"Thanks." Kody handed him the record.

The father walked over to little Dominic and rubbed the top of his head while looking at Dane. "You're the best." He smiled easily for the first time.

Dane shook the father's hand. "My pleasure."

As Dominic and his father walked away, several spectators stuffed money into the overflowing pitcher and voiced their appreciation. Once the crowd had begun to disperse, Kody emptied the pitcherful of cash into his guitar bag, intent on counting everything at the end of the day.

"Pretty good start," Dane said, stretching his neck.

Downplaying his pleasant surprise, Kody nonchalantly replied, "Yeah," while fishing sunglasses from his coat and putting them on. He wanted a cigarette, but not as badly as he wanted money. "Ready for another?"

Dane said, "Sure," and they jumped into the next song.

29

Kneeling, Kody opened his cash-filled guitar bag and took a victorious drag of his cigarette. The tie-dye vendor stuck her head out from between two technicolor onesies dangling from the tent. "You can't be smoking here."

Kody glared at her through his sunglasses.

"Put it out, or I'm calling the market master." She disappeared behind the clothes.

Kody mumbled and smeared the cigarette on the curb.

As the day wound down, vendors disassembled their booths while Dane, releasing a contemplative breath, surveyed the grounds with his hands in his shorts pockets. In front of him, an Indian man pushed a wooden cart stacked with beat-up plastic containers toward a blue van. Once the man had passed, Dane turned and glanced down at the money. "Damn. What a haul!"

Kody wanted to count the cash alone, and he searched for a way to get Dane to—

"Hey. While you split that up," Dane said, "I'm gonna see if those food trucks are still open."

Simple enough.

Dane sauntered toward the hangar, and Kody grabbed a handful of bills from the bag and sat on the curb. He separated the cash by denomination before fishing out another wad, then another. When the bag was emptied, there were a surprising amount of twenties, some tens, several fives, a huge stack of ones, and a handful of loose change, which he scooped from the bottom of the bag and stuffed into his jeans.

"Young man," a female voice spoke from behind.

Kody looked over his shoulder at the woman who had been selling acrylic paintings. Wayward gray hairs danced in the gentle breeze. "I think it's so sweet, what you two did for that little boy earlier."

Kody nodded.

The woman's eyes radiated wisdom, glowing orbs of truth. "I had a much better day than I'd hoped for, happened to sell a couple of originals." She nodded toward the empty space where her booth had been set up. "So I want you to take this." She handed Kody a hundred-dollar bill. "And see to it that your partner gets his share."

Behind the sunglasses, Kody's eyes fixed hungrily on the money.

"If you knew how much I made today, you wouldn't think twice about it."

Kody glanced toward the hangar. *No sign of Dane.* He refocused on the woman and took the bill. "Thanks."

"Keep sharing your art." The woman indicated the space around her. "The world needs it more than you know."

She turned and limped across the grass, shrinking gradually until she was smaller than Kody's thumbnail. As she moved along the edge of the pond, she passed a man patting his hands on his knees. In the water before the man, a golden retriever swam, tennis ball in mouth, toward the shore. It emerged from the pond and shook itself vigorously, spraying drops in every direction. The dog spat the ball onto the grass and gazed expectantly at its owner with pink tongue dangling from its mouth. The owner bent to grab the ball, straightened his posture, and cocked his arm back. The retriever fixed its eyes on the yellow projectile, and, when the owner flung his arm in an overhead arc, the dog bolted across the grass.

From Kody's vantage point, he could see that the owner hadn't actually thrown the ball but had instead kept it hidden behind his back. The dog, running excitedly back and forth, searched the grass, glancing sporadically at its owner for a hint, clue, or command.

Running around, Kody thought, *searching for something, only to discover that what we were chasing was never there in the first place.*

The man threw the ball, and, as the retriever bolted ecstatically, Kody inspected the hundred-dollar bill in his hand, turning it over, admiring the iridescent stripe that ran from top to bottom. He looked toward the hangar, where Dane was leaning against a food truck, eating a sandwich.

He seems content, Kody reasoned. *How badly could he really need the money?*

The Feeling began to swell—dark and heavy, filling his stomach like liquid lead.

What did Dane do, anyways? I played the guitar and sang. I chose the songs. Those records we sold were mine. In fact, if it wasn't for me, he wouldn't have even had the chance to play today.

The pressure mounted. His chest tightened.

I deserve it.

Kody stuffed the hundred-dollar bill into his pocket. Then he split up the remaining cash.

30

With the violin case slung about his shoulder and a wad of bills in his pocket, Dane strutted up to the entryway and pressed a button on the panel. Seconds later, a crude buzzer sounded, and he opened the door and trekked up a flight of creaky wooden stairs before following the ceiling-mounted piping down a long hallway. He knocked at room 207, and Risa shouted, "Come in!"

When Dane opened the door, the room was pitch black.

"Quick! Close it," Risa commanded from the darkness.

Stepping over the threshold, Dane shut the door and called out, "Marco."

Across the nothingness, a small dot of phosphorescent light appeared on the wall and began to crawl upward, leaving a trail of glowing green as it moved. After a few seconds, the trail had spelled, "POLO," and he heard a disembodied giggle as the luminous word hung suspended in the dark.

"How did you—"

A powerful flash illuminated the room, revealing a long work bench, several easels, and a tall set of metal shelves stacked with various art supplies. Before the flash, Risa had leapt into the air, throwing her arms out and kicking her legs behind her. Now, the room was dark again, and Risa's silhouette—complete with wild curls—had been captured mid-jump and lingered as a black shadow on a large, yellow-green rectangle of glow-in-the-dark vinyl mounted to the far wall.

"Ooooh," she said, admiring her work.

Dane set his instrument on the floor and jogged toward the phosphorescent wall. "Badass! I remember playing with one of these at a museum when I was a kid." He came up behind Risa, and, when she stuck her butt out forcibly, he slapped it and moved around beside her. Face bathed in green light, Risa glanced at him and beckoned with a finger. Dane leaned in and, as their lips touched, another flash lit the room, and Risa looked toward the glowing wall, where her mid-jump silhouette had been replaced by the shadow of a tall, shaggy man kissing a curly-haired girl.

"Aw!" She pinched Dane's chin. "So cute."

Dane smiled and pointed at the wall. "Did you make this?"

"No. I use the space to paint, but I split the rent with a photographer who made it for a project he was doing with his kids." She rubbed a palm across Dane's back. "He's taking it down in a few days, so I wanted to play with it before it's gone."

"Good idea." Dane noted the objects made visible by the glow-in-the-dark wall. "What does he use the room for?"

"He prints here." Risa gestured toward the work bench. "Look." She clicked a button, and a flash illuminated two large printers, surrounded by stacks of cardboard mattes and photo paper. When darkness returned, the silhouettes on the wall were two people looking in the same direction.

"The mad scientist's lab," Dane said.

"Yup." Risa's phone rang, and she set the flash trigger and laser pointer on the floor before walking toward the light switch. "He actually *is* a wacko, but he's also really talented." She turned the lights on and stooped to fish the phone from her bag. "How was playing with that guy today?"

"Good." Dane squinted as his eyes adjusted. "We hit the Mueller market for a couple hours."

Risa spoke absentmindedly while staring at the screen. "That's my favorite one around here." She silenced the ringer and dropped the phone into her bag.

"Yeah. I liked it too," Dane said. "Pretty cool how they turned an old airport into a neighborhood."

Risa sauntered toward Dane, her ankle-length maroon skirt draping her curves elegantly. "*You're* pretty cool." She wrapped her arms around his waist and looked up at him. "You guys make some money?"

Dane stroked Risa's bare arms. "A little bit. We split everything fifty-fifty, and I walked with enough to buy you dinner."

"Yeah?" Her eyes sparkled with surprise.

Dane nodded, and his gaze drifted to an easel behind Risa. "Oh, hold on now." He peeled her arms from around his waist and stepped past her, walking toward a painting in progress.

"Don't look at that!" Risa positioned herself between Dane and the piece. "It's not even close to done yet."

He leaned to the side, trying to get a peek. "A work of art is never really finished."

Risa stood on her tiptoes and spread her arms wide, blocking his view. "Well, this one is really, *really* not finished."

Dane ducked and lunged forward, lifting Risa over his shoulder like a fireman picking up a child in danger.

"Dane, no!" Risa hammered his back with her fists; the force of her hits modulated Dane's speech.

"Wo-o-o-oah." He spun around, bent down, and set Risa's feet on the floor before turning to look at the painting.

On either side of the canvas were vermillion sandstone cliffs, craggy and precipitous, towering above the crystalline blue of a winding river. Jet-black shadows accentuated the rugged texture of the rock, which had been shaped over millennia by wind and water. The wide *V* of sky, above the canyon walls, was untouched by paint and remained white above the vividly colored landscape.

Gazing at the piece, Dane felt a simultaneous satisfaction and yearning, as if the answer to some long-forgotten question lay encoded in the brushstrokes. After noticing a tattered photograph of the canyon scene clipped to the easel, Dane turned to Risa. "Do you realize how good this is?"

She stood with her back to him, arms folded, tapping a foot. "I'm so embarrassed right now."

Dane came up behind her and placed his hands on her shoulders. He tried to spin her around, but she resisted. "What are you embarrassed about?" He glanced over his shoulder at the painting. "That looks almost identical to the picture." The colors mesmerized him. "Actually, it looks—"

"Better than the picture." Risa wheeled around, raising an eyebrow. "Right? That's what you were going to say?"

Dane smiled at her. "Well, if it wasn't true I wouldn't—"

"Say it?"

Dane chuckled and wrapped his arms around her. "Will you stop?" He rocked side to side. "Why are you being so weird about this?"

Risa pressed her forehead against Dane's chest, speaking into his sternum. "I never show my paintings to anyone."

Dane released her and took a step back. "Why not?"

Risa shrugged. "I just do them for me." She glanced at the easel. "They're my meditation."

"Well, your meditation happens to be very impressive." Risa grew a bashful grin. "How many of these have you done?"

She sighed and pointed past Dane. "In the corner. Behind the curtain."

Dane crossed the wooden floor to a closet hidden by a thick velvet curtain, which he opened, revealing shelves stacked with canvases of various sizes. Along the closet's floor were larger paintings stored front-to-back like crackers in a plastic sleeve. Dane turned to glance at Risa, who now stood close behind.

"Here." She reached past him and carefully slid one of the larger canvases from the row, turning it sideways and leaning it against the others, facing outward.

The image centered around a woman, who resembled Risa, sitting on a concrete stoop in front of a brick townhouse. Her painted eyes shone with hard-won strength above a mouth that turned almost-imperceptibly upward at its edges. Seated at her feet, one on either side, were two little girls with dimpled smiles and red bows adorning their pulled-back curls.

Dane pointed at one of the children. "This is you."

Risa made a clicking noise and looked at him, tilting her head. "Oh, he's good."

"And that's home, huh?"

Risa nodded. "That's home. The Bronx."

"Little different than Texas."

"You're telling me."

Dane released a long breath and admired the painting in silence—the window into Risa's past. While he noted the intricate details of the faces, an idea struck.

"Hey." He turned toward Risa. "There were some painters selling their work at the market today. What if—"

Risa blew air through her closed lips, making a "Pfft" sound.

"I'm just saying—"

She shook her head and waved a dismissive hand.

"Okay. I'm not telling you to sell these, but I will say this." Dane pointed toward the portrait. "That's better than anything I saw down there today."

Risa touched Dane's arm and looked into his eyes. "You're sweet." She shuffled past him and returned the portrait to its place in the closet. "Goodnight, Mama."

"Speaking of the market." Dane fished the phone from his pocket. "I've gotta show you a video of us playing with this kid today." Risa shut the curtain and walked to his side. "You'll love it."

Taking the phone with both hands, Risa gasped when she saw little Dominic shaking his plastic egg to the beat. "Oh. My. Goodness." She paused between each word. "He's adorable." She focused on Dane. "Oh and look at you go. Mister sexy violin man." Mimicking Dane's stance, Risa spread her feet wide apart and swayed back and forth. "You look so happy." She watched the phone intently for a moment. "And that's the weird songwriter you were talking about." She pointed at the screen and cocked her head. "Does he always close his eyes like that when he sings?"

"Yeah. Like ninety percent of the time."

Risa put the speaker to her ear and nodded thoughtfully. "I can hear the hurt in his voice. Even on this song." She glanced at Dane. "You were right. The boy's got soul." Risa handed the phone back. "It takes some real demons to make 'Here Comes the Sun' sound sad."

Dane stuffed the phone back into his pocket. "Dude's got something dark going on, for sure." He rubbed a palm along the side of his neck. "Pretty tough to be around too. Always seems to have his guard up. I tried getting him to grab a drink after we finished today, but he wasn't into it."

"Maybe he's just shy."

"Could be." Dane shrugged. "I'll give it another shot tomorrow. He asked me to come play at this winery in the hill country. So, if you're into it, I was thinking we could do that before going to my buddy's place for that campfire. I'll ask Kody if he wants to come with us after the gig. Maybe he'll loosen up under the stars."

"Mmmm." Risa took a step closer. "I'm excited to sit by the fire with you."

"I think you'll like Deven too."

"He's a glassblower who lives on a horse ranch. In a shack," Risa said. "What's not to like?"

Dane grinned softly. "So you're down for checking that gig out beforehand?"

"You said the place has wine?"

Dane nodded, and Risa squeezed his hand. "I'd love that." She kissed his cheek, skipped to the switch, and killed the lights. The glow-in-the-dark wall radiated like the entrance to some intergalactic portal. "Close your eyes."

Dane did as he was told, and, after several seconds of shuffling, he heard a flash.

"Wait." Risa came up behind Dane and positioned him so he faced the lucent wall. "Okay. Open."

The silhouette's elbows were bent. One hand was lost in a mess of feral hair, while the other rested on a hip that popped out above Risa's toned legs, which rose from the floor toward curvaceous hips and the inward dip of Risa's waist. Above this, a shapely breast was topped by a perky nipple.

"You're the hottest naked shadow I've ever seen."

Risa whispered from behind. "And you're a *real* poet." She reached around to unbutton Dane's shorts. "Okay." She lowered his zipper. "Your turn."

When Kody woke to the jackhammer the following morning, he saw a text from Red.

Call me when you have a moment.

Kody slid the curtain aside, opened the door, and stepped barefoot onto the gravel. Nearby, standing beside the chain-link fence, was a teenage girl holding the leash of a chihuahua peeing on a shrub. She turned to look at Kody, and her eyes widened.

"Oh, hey ..." Kody searched for words that would make him appear non-threatening despite having just emerged from the back of a van. The girl scooped up the dog, marched across the parking lot, and disappeared between two buildings. Wondering if he'd need to find a new place to park, Kody traversed the gravel, careful not to step on anything sharp or slimy. Once behind a dumpster, he pissed on the fence, thinking of the dog.

After his morning cigarette, he sat on a rock and called Red.

"Hey, Kody."

"Hi, Red. Saw your text."

"Yeah. Checking in about the session."

"Coming up," Kody replied. "Looking forward to it."

"Same." Red took a sip of something. "We've got an issue with Alyssa though. Her mother is sick, and she needs to fly out. She won't be back in time to track."

"Okay."

"I'm going to send you the names of some other fiddlers, so I'd like you to take some time today and check them out. Then get back to me, and we can lock down a replacement player."

Kody thought about Dane. *If I can get him on the recording, maybe I can stay with him while I'm in Nashville.* Another idea slithered in. *I may even be able to get him to play for free, save a couple hundred bucks ...*

"Actually," Kody said. "I met a guy down here who's from Nashville. We busked yesterday. Solid player. If you're open to it, I'd like to use him."

"Well." Red paused. "Is he going to be in town next week?"

"I think so."

There was a long silence before Red replied. "I'll want to hear him play. And I'll need to talk to him too. Have him send me a few clips or, better yet, a video, and we can go from there."

"Okay."

"The sooner the better."

"Got it."

"All right, Kody."

After hanging up, Kody glanced at the van. The front bumper was splattered with dead bugs and mud was streaked across the white paint around the wheel wells. Kody thought about washing the vehicle. Then he thought about washing himself.

Cautiously, he navigated the gravel and reached beneath the van to grab his shoes, which he turned upside down and shook vigorously to clear out any spiders that may have spent the night. After sitting on the running board and picking rocks from the bottoms of his feet, Kody put his shoes on and closed the sliding door before going around and climbing onto the driver's seat. He started the van and drove to Stanley's, where he parked along the curb in front of the house. Grabbing his backpack, he headed to the front door and knocked.

"Come in!"

Kody opened the door and crossed the dirty carpet to the computer room, where Stanley sat at his desk. On one screen, Kody saw a logo, mid-design. On the other, a woman was bent over with a large, muscular man thrusting from behind. The man grimaced, sweating. Stanley clicked the mouse and dragged part of the logo, enlarging it as Kody's eyes darted between the two screens. He glanced over his shoulder, toward the door.

"What's up, Kody?" Stanley was focused on his work.

Kody cleared his throat.

The mouse clicked. "Bathroom's all yours."

"Um—"

Stanley spun in his chair and studied Kody. "What?"

Kody focused on the second screen, where the woman was now on her knees.

Stanley pointed over his shoulder. "Oh, this?" He turned his head to watch.

Kody slid a hand into a pocket of the long black coat.

"I'll tell you what." Stanley looked at Kody. "If a man can't appreciate this, I don't want to know him."

The woman wiped her face.

"You got a problem with it?"

Kody fingered the pepper spray. "Nope." He produced a ten-dollar bill and left it on the desk as he rushed past, headed toward the hallway.

"Kody."

He wheeled around.

"I thought you'd be into it."

Kody nodded once. "It's great."

Stanley smirked, and Kody trudged down the hall. While closing the bath-room door, he made a note to himself: *Tomorrow, bring the knife.*

Dane opened his eyes to see Risa lying inches away with both hands folded beneath her cheek. Seeing him wake, she gasped softly. "There he is." She pinched Dane's nose, and, when he smiled, Risa poked at his dimple. "Did you dream?" She propped herself up with a pillow and the blanket slid down her bare brown skin.

Dane shook his head and reached out to pull Risa closer. "You?"

She settled onto Dane's chest and traced a lazy finger across his stomach. "I did." Dane felt the vibrations in his ribcage as Risa spoke. "I dreamt I was on the beach in California. It was sunny and beautiful, and I was wet from playing in the waves. I was laying on a towel, and my skin was all warm and salty. Then I looked up into the blue sky, and there was a hole." Risa looked at him. "It was so strange—a black hole in the blue sky. And I stared at it for a while, then I sat up so I could watch the ocean and the people playing in the water. Oh! There was this little boy and his mom. They were making a sandcastle, and the boy was so cute.

"But then I looked back up at the sky, and the hole was bigger. It wasn't growing, but it was bigger than before. So I laid back down and closed my eyes, and when I opened them, I hoped the hole would be gone, but this time it took up most of the sky."

Risa rubbed her cold toes against Dane's foot. "I got scared and looked around, but the beach was still bright, and everyone was still happy. But every time I'd look up, there was just this big darkness." Risa rolled onto her stomach and rested her chin on Dane's chest, playing with the hairs. "I don't know what it means, or if it means anything at all. You know, sometimes dreams try to tell you things." She sighed. "But I think I was the only one who could see the darkness. 'Cuz I looked around, and everyone was laughing, and playing, and enjoying their day, so I didn't want to talk to them about it. I didn't want to ruin their fun." She gazed deep into Dane's eyes. "But I couldn't stop thinking about it."

Risa was in her apartment, getting ready, while Dane sat on a lounge chair by the pool. Resting his hands behind his head, he closed his eyes behind sunglasses and savored the sensation of warm solar fingers massaging his cheeks and forehead. This melanin-making bliss was accentuated by a bouncy reggae rhythm which *ticka-ticka*'d through his phone's speaker. After a long moment spent thoughtlessly floating, he eased an eye open. In the shallow end, a young mother stood with her hands on her hips as her toddler girl—wearing goggles and water wings—splashed and giggled. The reggae stopped as Dane's phone rang. Languidly, he lifted it, glanced at the screen, and answered, "Hey, Kody."

"Do you have a second?"

"Yeah." Dane sat up. "What's going on?"

"Red called this morning. Sounds like the fiddler we had scheduled can't make the session. So I pitched the idea of you filling in, and Red seemed open to it."

Dane tilted his head back and closed his eyes. The sun's hands worked their magic. "Are you messing with me?"

After a pause, Kody said, "No."

"That's *awesome*!" Dane's outburst startled the mother and girl, who looked in his direction.

He raised an apologetic hand and quieted his voice. "That's awesome, Kody. When's the recording?"

"You'll need to reach out to Red first. I'll send you his email. He wants to hear you play before committing, so get him a few videos or sound clips."

Dane was stricken with disbelief, thinking of the many successful bands Red had produced. "All right. I'll shoot those out to him ASAP."

"One more thing," Kody said.

"What's that?"

"I don't know anyone in Nashville." He paused. "You stay in the RV when you're up there, right?"

Dane chuckled. "Man, you get me a session with Red fucking Smith, and I'll give you the thing."

Kody was silent.

"I'm joking," Dane said. "But you can totally stay in the rig as long as you need to. I've got a loft bed above the cockpit with your name on it."

"Okay," Kody replied. "It has a shower too?"

"That's right. No need for you to pay some Craigslist killer to use his."

There was a short pause. "I'll send Red's info now."

Two terrestrial hands rested on Dane's shoulders, and the thumbs began to move in firm circles. Dane reached up to stroke Risa's arm. "Thanks a ton, Kody. See you tonight."

Risa rested a cheek on Dane's head. "Thanks a *ton*?"

The reggae resumed, and Dane turned the volume down, resting the phone on the chair. He took Risa's wrist, guided her around, and scooted to the side so she could sit. "You remember that song we danced to in Nashville, in the rain?"

Risa broke into a deep southern twang, *"I wonder how it'd feel to be your man."*

"That's the one." Dane smiled. "The guy who recorded it is named Red Smith."

Risa nodded.

"The guy's got, like, ten Grammys under his belt, excellent producer." Dane flicked his hand. "Anyway, Kody is recording with him next week and—"

"How?"

"Red's brother saw Kody play and connected them."

"Lucky Kody," Risa said.

"Yeah, well, lucky me too."

Risa's eyes widened, and she clutched Dane's thigh. "Why?"

"Sounds like the fiddle player who was going to record had to cancel, and—"

Risa squeaked and threw her arms around Dane, cuddling him as if she were a supportive koala. "And *you're* going to play instead!"

Dane laughed and rubbed a hand across her back. "Hopefully. I have to send Red a video so he can hear me. If he likes it, *then* I'll get the gig."

Risa searched Dane's eyes. "I knew you had something special." She grabbed Dane through his shorts. "Besides this."

He pulled her in, and the kiss lasted only a few seconds before the mother in the pool cleared her throat forcibly. Disapproval echoed through the courtyard.

Snapped out of their moment, Dane and Risa looked at the woman, who stood in the shallow end with arms crossed, glowering at the couple. The little girl was mimicking her mother's discontent, bobbing in the water with tiny brows furrowed.

"That's freaking adorable." Risa glanced at Dane and gave him one more south-of-the-beltline squeeze. "Let's go inside."

34

That afternoon, Risa and Dane decided to head to the hill country for a swim in some springs. They packed a bag with bathing suits and towels, and Dane grabbed his violin and a change of clothes for the gig that night. On their way out of the apartment, Risa got a phone call. After digging into her bag to check the screen, she promptly silenced the ringer and locked the door.

They traversed the winding path that led from Risa's building to the street. As they approached her Subaru, which was parked along the curb, her pulse accelerated, and she glanced at Dane, who hadn't noticed yet.

"What's this place called again?" Dane asked.

"Krause Springs." She braced herself as they stopped in front of the vehicle.

A long quiet fell between them before Dane gestured toward the Subaru and said, "I wish I'd thought of that."

Risa walked to the windshield and raised the wiper, removing the folded note and pink rose from beneath. She turned to Dane with an apologetic look. "Okay. I have to talk to you about something."

"You don't have to explain."

"No," Risa said. "I want to."

They sat on the curb, and Risa laid the note and flower on the ground. "For the last few months, I've been seeing someone. I didn't think it was serious, but, well ..." Risa gestured toward the gifts.

Dane chuckled. "Yeah. Look, we just met, so—"

"No. I don't want you to think I've got some rotating cast of guys here. I was just seeing this one, Vithu, from time to time, but I never thought it would become anything. He'd just reach out every few weeks, and we'd have drinks and hang out. But there was never any connection there." Risa poked a vein on Dane's hand. "But, since you've been in town, and I've been unavailable, he's been calling me every day." She shook her head. "It's so strange, Dane. He wasn't acting like this at *all* before. I mean ..." She lifted the flower and dropped it. "Really?"

Dane grinned. "Pretty classy."

"The point I'm trying to make is I *feel* something with you." Risa scanned Dane's blue eyes. "And I didn't really want to have this talk, 'cuz I don't know what you're thinking about all of this. But I can't pretend I don't love spending time with you." She rubbed the back of Dane's head. "And I know you like to travel, and bounce around, and be and do whatever, so I don't want you to feel any pressure to change that." Risa withdrew her hand. "But I just have to let you know where I'm at."

Dane nodded. "I have a great time with you too. Definitely an intense connection." He squeezed Risa's leg. "And not to mention, you're a complete and total babe."

She smiled, thinking, *Go on.*

"But we've still got a few days together," Dane said. "How 'bout we talk at the end of the trip and see where we're at?"

Risa hoped this wasn't Dane's way of dodging the conversation that had been so skillfully avoided by other men in her past. Summoning her poker face, she raised her chin. "Sounds like a plan."

"Cool." He nodded toward the note. "Now lemme read it."

Risa punched his knee.

They stood and got into the Subaru, and Risa tossed the note and flower into the back. When she started the engine, tender acoustic music blasted from the speakers. Giggling, she turned the volume down. "Whoops."

"You were rocking out."

"Busted."

As they pulled from the curb, a gray sedan accelerated from behind, closing in on the Subaru's bumper. Checking the rearview, Risa's throat tightened as she recognized the car and its scowling driver.

No way.

She gripped the wheel.

Dane turned to look through the back window. "What's with this asshole?"

"That's him." Risa pressed the gas, hurrying along the car-lined street.

"Him?" Dane asked. "Rose guy?"

Ignoring a stop sign, Risa turned right, speeding up. The sedan was on them.

"Pull over here," Dane pointed toward the curb. "I'll talk to him."

"It won't be a *talk*."

"I'll handle it, either way."

There was a green light ahead, and Risa eased off the gas until it turned yellow. At the last second, she slammed her foot down, blasting through the intersection. Vithu's sedan screeched to a halt as Risa's Subaru rocketed up the street and went left, then right. She pulled into an alley between two shops and veered into a paved lot. Once parked, she pressed her forehead against the steering wheel and covered her face with both hands, trying to calm her rapid breathing.

Dane placed a palm on Risa's back.

"What a *creep*!" Risa yelled into the wheel.

Dane stroked softly.

"I don't know what's gotten into him!" She looked at Dane. "Before, it was almost impossible to get him to hang out. Now, he's *stalking* me?"

Risa's phone rang, and Dane reached into her bag.

"Dane. No!" She yanked his arm from the bag and grabbed the phone, answering, "What the fuck, Vithu!"

A beat of silence. Then a concerned voice said, "Reesy?"

Risa rubbed her brow and sighed. "Hi, Mom."

Dane laughed, and Risa pointed a finger at him, trying not to smile while mouthing, "Shut up."

35

Kody spread the legs of a speaker stand and positioned it on a corner of the wooden platform that would serve as a stage. In front of the platform, a lawn sprawled out with several tables and chairs, most of which were occupied by prattling people with glasses of wine. Beyond the makeshift stage, the land dropped, revealing the verdant hills of Spicewood. As far as one could see, oak and ashe juniper crowded together, pushing their branches outward, fighting for space beneath the sapphire sky. The smell of *asado* wafted through the air from a large grill on a wooden deck. An Argentinian man, wearing a grease-stained apron, carried two plates of juicy steak and blackened vegetables to a table where a pair of women scooted a bottle of syrah to make room. Dane eyed the meat as he and Risa walked by. "Damn," he said. "That smells phenomenal."

"Phe-nom-e-nal." Risa counted the syllables on her fingers. "Good word."

Dane grinned as they approached Kody, who slid a speaker onto its stand.

"Hey, bud," Dane greeted.

Kody, wearing a black, collared button-up, secured the speaker and inspected Dane's outfit: swim trunks and a T-shirt. "Did you bring a change of clothes?"

Dane shot Risa a smirking glance. "Yeah, man." He looked at Kody. "We just got done swimming." He patted his backpack. "Got 'em in here."

Kody bent to grab a mic stand.

"I want you to meet Risa," Dane said.

Kody glanced at her and said mechanically, "Hello, Risa."

She forced a smile and waved. "Looking forward to hearing you play."

"Hopefully it's worth the anticipation." Kody adjusted the mic stand.

After a long silence, Dane indicated the building across the lawn. "Well, I'm gonna head over there and change."

Kody checked his phone. "We're on in thirty."

Dane nodded. "Does this place give their hard-working musicians some wine?"

"I don't drink during the performance."

Risa suppressed a giggle.

"But," Dane countered with a grin. "If you happened to have a fiddle player who *did* like to partake—"

"Can you hold it together?" Kody snapped.

"I'm a big boy, Kody. I can handle a little red."

"All right." Kody slid the mic into the clip. "Tell Bruce you're with the band."

Dane nodded, and he and Risa started across the lawn. Once out of earshot, she said, "My god. You weren't exaggerating at *all*." Risa waved her hands on either side of her head, doing her best Kody. *"Can you hold it together?"* She scoffed. "What a dick."

"Yeah." Dane shook his head. "He *is* making this Nashville thing happen though ..."

"And that's worth it?"

They approached the quaint building, where Dane opened the door and held it for her. "I've put up with much worse for a lot less." The tasting room was small with a sizable window that revealed a sturdy oak with a wooden swing. "Plus," Dane said, following her inside. "I think there's a decent guy in there somewhere."

Risa whipped around and raised an eyebrow.

"I do," he reiterated. "And after the gig, we'll have Kody over to the ranch, get him drunk, and see if I'm right."

Risa grasped Dane's arm. "I don't know if he should come."

"Worst case scenario." Dane poked at her navel ring. "He gets huffy and leaves."

"And best?"

Dane winked. "We'll write a hit."

36

Risa sipped her cabernet and admired the sky ahead, which looked as though the gods had used enormous brushes to paint psychedelic streaks across the darkening horizon. In front of the masterpiece, Kody and Dane were seated, performing beneath a strand of bulbs dangling between two trees. A choir of crickets chirped, accompanying Kody who, with eyes closed, sang in a near-whisper.

"What I thought were the stars,

Turned out to be the light that shone out from behind the bars.

And what I thought was the sea,

I watched it turn to sand right in front of me."

The small crowd sat entranced as a soft breeze swayed the lights, the reflections of which danced across the makeshift stage as Kody sang the next verse.

"What I thought was my voice,

It crept into my ears and left me with a choice.

It wiped the smile from my face.

And now my stomach turns with the thought of this food on my plate."

Dane's violin swelled as Kody's strumming intensified.

"I'm reaching for the other side of me."

Kody crooned a series of *"O-Oohs,"* which sounded to Risa like some Native American chant, rhythmic and hypnotic.

"I'm reaching for the other side of me."

A man at a nearby table began to speak but was silenced by his wife.

"O-Ooh. O-Ooh. O-Ooh."

Both players eased up on their instruments, lowering the volume and tempering the music's intensity.

"There's a light up ahead. You take the road right here, and I'll take the one on the left.

Oh, I'll miss you, my friend. I loved the time we had. I'm so sad that it has to end."

Dane dragged his bow across the strings, sprouting goose bumps across Risa's skin as the night seeped like thick oil across the sky's vibrant canvas. Kody's voice jumped an octave, trembling with painful recollection.

"Oh, when I get afraid, I'll close my eyes and I'll think of the mem'ries we made.

Of that smile on your face. The one you wore when we made this world our perfect place."

He held the last note, transforming it into a series of haunting *"O-Oohs,"* and the intensifying pressure in Risa's sinuses caused her eyes to water.

"I'm reaching for the other side of me. So I can find another side of meee."
Dane's fiddle soared, harmonizing with Kody's sorrowful moans.
"O-Ooh. O-Ooh. O-Ooh."
The music slowed as Kody sang the final line.
"I'm reaching for the other side ... of ... me."
The notes dwindled to silence, and Kody opened his eyes, staring over the heads of the audience. Wiping a tear from her cheek, Risa searched Kody's gaze, and her stomach wrenched. Set like hot coals in the middle of Kody's blank expression, his eyes—burning with some insatiable hunger—resembled those of a stray dog. Those eyes fixed nervously on Risa, who averted her attention and set her drink down to join the applause.

"Y'all know any Willie?" a plump white man blurted. "He lives just down the road. Maybe you turn up a bit, and he'll hear ya and come pick a few."

Dane began to pluck the melody to Willie Nelson's "On the Road Again" while tilting his head rhythmically from side to side. Some people chuckled, and Kody shook his head. "Don't know it."

"Aw, come on, guy," the man said. "It's just a couple easy chords."

"Come up and play it then." Kody invited the man with a finger.

The man laughed, but when he saw that Kody wasn't joking, he said, "Oh, hey, guy. I was just playin' around." He tugged at the waist of his jeans. "Didn't mean to step on yer cock."

The crowd murmured, and Dane called out, "Hey! How 'bout some Townes Van Zandt?"

Jutting out his bottom lip, the man nodded in approval. "Where'd you boys say you were from?"

Dane replied, "I've lived all over. Nashville now, but I'm originally from California."

Kody said, "Portland."

"And you heard about ol' Townes all the way out there?"

"A good song's a good song," Dane said.

"California." The man pointed at Dane. "I'm not a fan of your state—looney politics and all—but you've got good taste in music. And you play the hell outta that fiddle."

The crowd began to chatter impatiently.

"Townes, it is," Kody said, clamping a capo across his strings.

"Cool." Dane readied his instrument. "Oh, wait. One more thing." He scanned the crowd, whose faces were illuminated by the strand of lights. Kody cleared his throat forcibly. "What's the difference between a violin and a fiddle?" The audience fell silent with anticipation. "A violin has strings." Dane readied his bow. "And a fiddle has *strangs*!" He played a cheesy run over a few half-hearted laughs.

Risa looked downward and pressed a palm over her eyes.

After a *chucka-chucka* on the guitar, Kody strummed an up-tempo progression and Dane joined in. The large man—stepping to the beat like a dancing cartoon bear—grooved toward the open suitcase, which sat on a stool near the stage. He dropped a twenty into the tip pitcher and lifted his hat to the boys.

Looking past the man, with her mind floating on the music, Risa noticed a solitary star twinkling in the darkening sky. She lifted the glass to her lips and saw herself as that star—out on her own, far away from her family and most of her friends. The cabernet danced across Risa's tongue as she thought about her mother, about how badly she missed being able to hug her. She remembered her father's deep, comforting voice and her sister's obnoxious laugh ...

But, glancing around at the people on the lawn, Risa was proud of herself for going for it, for taking the travel job. The idea of leaving her hospital and New York had terrified her. Yet as she breathed the sultry Texas air and watched Dane—so passionate and immersed in expression—Risa understood why that lone star was burning so brightly.

37

The owner of the winery stacked chairs on the deck as the remaining patrons meandered toward their vehicles. Dane, seated at a table with Risa, told her he'd be back and walked across the lawn to Kody, who was wrapping a microphone cable. "You need help with this stuff?"

"I got it." Kody dropped the coiled cable onto the stage and bent to pick up another.

"Hey."

Kody looked at Dane.

"That was a really good show tonight, man. People were feeling it."

Kody straightened his posture and shook his head. "I can't believe I forgot the second verse to 'Paradise.'"

"We're always our own worst critics," Dane replied. "I bet no one even noticed."

"I did."

Dane huffed and looked over his shoulder at Risa, who was talking with a woman at an adjacent table. "Dude." He refocused on Kody. "You're too hard on yourself." Kody started to speak, but Dane held up a hand. "Hold on. Let me finish." He nodded toward Kody. "You probably *know* you're hella critical, but I don't know if anyone else has ever told you that. And I don't know if it'll make a difference to you or not, but I'm gonna say this too: you're super talented. And every time I've seen you perform, people have responded to that." He pointed. "But it doesn't seem like you take the time to enjoy the good things your talent is bringing."

Kody eyed the wine glass in Dane's hand.

"I know I've had a few," Dane said. "But I would've told you this either way." He poked at Kody's shoulder. "You need to have some *fun*, bud." Dane gestured at the space around them. "I mean look at this place." Crickets chirped in the balmy night. "This was our office. We were *paid* to be here."

Kody surveyed the property, thinking back to his warehouse job, remembering how much he had hated the alarm clock telling him what to do. Dragging himself out the door only to unload boxes from a delivery truck in the freezing rain.

"You made this happen," Dane continued. "You chose this. And it's been an awesome experience."

Kody watched the owner collect glasses from a table. "There *are* worse jobs."

Dane slapped Kody's arm. "Hell yeah, there are!"

Kody grimaced.

"Sorry, man. Didn't mean to hit that hard. Just got stoked to hear you say it."

Risa stepped onto the stage and stood beside Dane, who put an arm around her and looked at Kody. "Hey, so, Risa and I are headed to my buddy's place after this. He's a glass artist who lives on a horse ranch a few miles away."

Kody knew where this was headed.

"We're gonna make a bonfire and have a few drinks, probably play some music." Dane gestured toward Kody. "You should come, man." He indicated the parking lot. "You could even park the van at Deven's and crash for the night. If nothing else, it'll be a quiet place to sleep."

Kody imagined waking up without the sound of a jackhammer. "Is there a shower?"

Dane shook his head. "He's allergic to water."

Kody stared vacantly.

"Of course they have a shower." Dane picked up a speaker, smiling assuredly. "I'll give you a hand, and you can follow us over there."

IV

The Big Darkness

38

"What was your name for this?" Risa asked.

She, Dane, and Kody stood beside a steel table in the barn. The glass artist, Deven, wore thick goggles that hugged his dark skin as he stuck a metal rod into the crucible's fiery maw and dipped its end into a soup of molten glass. "A titty hit," he answered.

Kody glanced toward a glass wine tumbler, overturned on the table with a dime-sized hole in the bottom.

About the size of a B-cup.

Deven pulled the end of the rod—encased in glowing goo—from the oven and lowered it, touching the table. When he lifted the rod, a small glob of incandescent liquid remained on the steel surface. "Okay." He set the rod aside and fished a tiny plastic bag from his overalls. After opening the bag, he pinched a marble-sized bud of marijuana from the cluster and scanned the group. "Who's first?"

Risa, Dane, and Kody considered the cooling blob. "Is that safe?" Kody asked.

"Do it all the time," Deven replied.

Dane chuckled. "Yeah. So, like he said, is it safe?"

Risa stepped forward. "I'll do it."

"There you go, Risa." Deven pointed at Dane. "Show these boys what's up."

Deven set the bud of marijuana on the glob of hot glass and nodded toward the overturned tumbler with the air-flow hole. "Take that and cover the weed up."

Risa lifted the tumbler and lowered it, upside down, over the pot-topped blob, creating a drug-smoking snow globe.

"Now plug the hole."

She used a finger, and the inside of the wine tumbler grew hazy as the gob of hot glass caused the marijuana to burn.

"Hit it whenever."

Risa held her curls back with her free hand, bent forward, and removed her finger from the hole before pressing her lips to it. Tilting the tumbler, she sucked the smoke, and the resulting cough expelled a thick white cloud. After catching her breath, she laughed with a "Woo!" as Dane rubbed a palm up and down her back.

"Like a champ," Deven said. He indicated the tumbler and looked at Kody. "You want next?"

Kody eyed the wisp of smoke that rose from the smoldering bud. "I don't know if—"

"Kody," Dane interrupted. "How many chances will you get to do something like this?"

Kody thought about the last time he'd smoked weed, when he had panicked and walked the streets of downtown Portland until he felt better. He also remembered how, after that, he had locked himself in his room and written what he considered to be one of his best songs. Stepping forward, he decided to take the chance that the latter might repeat itself.

"My man," Deven said.

Kody plugged the hole with a thumb, and the tumbler became cloudy. Stooping, he put his mouth to the opening and let the smoke fill his lungs. Upon releasing the smoldering breath, a rush of fearful regret swept over him, and his mouth went dry. To numb the oncoming sensations, he took a comforting swig of beer.

"Oh, wow." Risa grinned widely and shuddered, wrapping her arms around Dane. "I'm all tingly."

Dane ran a hand through her hair. "I'm gonna get tingly with you."

"Lemme get you a new one." Deven picked up the rod and stuck it in the oven.

Watching this, Kody's sense of time distorted. Minutes and seconds expanded, leaving room for more swirling thoughts. He glanced at Dane and Risa, who were embracing, and the Thing coiled tightly inside. A scene from years ago wormed to the surface of his psyche: she and Kody were seated on the grass, hand in hand. The band they loved was playing the song that had punctuated their first road trip together. As her thumb moved back and forth across his clammy palm, the band's lyrics created a tremendous pressure behind the cracked dam inside Kody. At first, his tears came slowly, silently. Soon, he was sobbing uncontrollably, his head buried into her shoulder as she stroked his hair and whispered words of affirmation.

This was the last night they would spend together.

Snapping back, Kody focused on the oven's orange glow, reflected in Deven's dark goggles. A cold, prickling sensation rippled outward from Kody's chest, and he fixed his gaze on the crucible of hot glass. Suddenly, as if under the influence of some terrible gravity, Kody's attention was sucked back into himself, and he felt the inescapable desire to rip the skin from his bones and run screaming into the night. Sipping from the bottle as though it were an antidote, Kody became aware of the fact that, should someone speak to him, he might not be able to respond in a socially acceptable manner.

He decided that, rather than risk losing control of himself or behaving foolishly, he would leave until his mind returned to a familiar state. As Deven maneuvered the rod out of the oven and left a fresh, glowing blob on the table, Kody said, "I'll be back," and walked outside.

When Dane found Kody, he was standing near the pasture fence, staring at the night sky with his hands in the pockets of his long black coat.

"Thinking about the meaning of life?" Dane asked.

Kody whipped around. "There is no meaning." He ran a hand through his hair, as though the gesture might retract his statement. "Why do we do it?"

"Life?" Dane noticed an unfamiliar looseness in Kody. "Why do we do what?"

"Anything." Kody kicked at the grass. "But, more specifically, art. Why do we even bother?"

"Well." Dane turned and leaned against the fence, gazing across the property at Risa and Deven, who were seated beside a campfire. "Other than it just being fun, I play music because it's a way for me to connect with the world, with people. I guess it's a way for me to give them something of value."

Kody tilted his head. "*Is* it valuable?"

This was the first time Dane had seen Kody smile. It reminded him of an alligator baring its teeth, preparing to attack. "Damn." Dane chuckled. "That pot really got you, didn't it?"

The smile submerged.

"All right." Dane flattened his tone. "I think art *is* valuable. Take tonight, for example. All those people at the winery really enjoyed what we were doing. Our show gave them a new memory, a cool way to spend their evening." He pointed. "Shit. One of your songs even made Risa cry."

The smirk that attempted to cross Kody's face was promptly beaten into submission.

"I think that's worth something," Dane added.

Leaning against the fence, Kody glanced at his feet, muttering unintelligibly. "Huh?"

"I don't care about people's memories," he repeated before fixing his gaze on Dane. "I don't like people." He shook his head. "In fact, I think I hate them."

Dane laughed as if he were reacting to a child's ridiculous comment.

Kody's eyes flared.

"Really?" Dane said. "You *hate* people? Why?"

"I ..." Kody paused. "I try very hard to see what I'm supposed to see in them." He glanced at Dane as though he may be punished for what he was about to say. "But beneath all the surface-level pleasantries, the where-did-you-grow-ups and conversations about the weather, beyond people asking, 'How are you?' without ever wanting an honest answer, past all that hollow, energy-wasting bullshit, I can't help but see us for what we actually are."

"And what's that?"

"We're the problem."

"The problem?" Dane said. "The problem with what?"

"*The* problem." Kody gestured frustratedly. "We're fucking everything up."

Dane searched Kody's face. "You mean, like, the environment?"

"That's a big part of it."

"Well ..." Dane worked to formulate a response. "I guess things are pretty bad right now, but—"

"Listen." Kody pushed off the fence and turned to face Dane. "Since the beginning of humankind, all we've done is destroy. Everywhere our species has gone, we've consumed resources, decimated habitat, and driven other animals to extinction, rapidly. And now ..." Kody opened his hands. "We're killing everything more efficiently than ever, including ourselves. And we're pretending we have the power to *do* something about it. Like we're going to impact the future by not using plastic bags or straws, or by driving electric cars instead of using gas. But we won't change anything. Because what the world really needs is less of *us*." Kody pointed between them. "We're a disease. A cancer. A malignant bacteria having an identity crisis. Our nature, our purpose, is to annihilate this planet and everything on it. And we're trying to convince ourselves that we're the guardians and shepherds of the same organism we're programmed to destroy!" Kody scoffed. "Think about it." He nodded toward Dane. "What feels good?"

Dane scratched his head. "Damn, dude." He paused. "That's more words than you've said since we met." He crossed his arms. "What do you mean?"

"The first thing that comes to mind when you hear that question. What feels good?"

Dane played along. "Sex."

"All right. Do you know why?"

Dane grinned. "I can give you a few reasons."

"Yeah, but what's the biological reason?"

Dane waited.

"Sex feels good," Kody explained, "because it's the single most important function we, as infectious organisms, can perform. Reproduce, perpetuate the species. We're hardwired to want that feeling because it spreads our disease."

Dane inhaled slowly, wishing Kody would go back to being quiet. "Okay."

"What else?" Kody asked.

Dane cocked his head to the side.

"What *else* feels good?"

Hoping to end the conversation, Dane said, "Farting."

"How about that human connection you mentioned?"

Dane was disappointed that his joke didn't get a reaction. But, considering his audience, he wasn't surprised. "Kody, I know what you're doing here. And no matter what I say, you're going to find some way to bring it back to humanity killing the world. So, honestly, I don't even want to bother."

"Does this not make sense to you?" Kody asked.

Dane gazed up at the stars, thinking about how each one was like the sun, perhaps shining light and life upon distant worlds. "Nope."

"Well, it's pretty simple. Maybe I can try to explain it differently."

Dane waved a hand and shook his head. "We're good, man. Let's just forget about it." He looked at Kody. "Out of curiosity, though, what were you gonna say about human connection?"

Kody spoke matter-of-factly, "Connection feels good because it helps us coordinate, unifies us, two or more bacteria, making the infection spread more efficiently."

Dane smirked, and Kody said, "What?"

"What happened to you, then?"

"What do you mean?"

Dane nodded toward Kody. "You say it's in our nature to connect, and that we should feel good about that connection. So what happened with you? Thinking you hate people, not wanting to interact with them. Did your bacterial DNA miss the memo?"

Kody scanned Dane's face as he answered. "I don't think we're supposed to know what we are." He fidgeted with something in his coat pocket. "That's part of the way we're engineered, with some delusion of divine guidance. It's like our whole society is set up to keep us from thinking about the truth of our role, while at the same time speeding up the destruction itself."

Dane chuckled, and Kody's features hardened.

"Sorry man, didn't mean to laugh, but I heard something on a podcast the other day that relates to this, and it *is* kinda funny." Kody stopped fidgeting. His stare was like a pistol aimed at Dane, finger on the trigger. "It was a scientist talking about cancer, and he was saying that in order for a cell to become cancerous, all of its communication with surrounding cells needs to be cut off. It doesn't actually matter if there's no genetic mutation in the cell. Even a normal, healthy cell will still become cancerous if you fully isolate it from others."

Dane watched as Kody considered the subtext of his statement. "You mean by putting the cell alone in a petri dish?"

"No. Something about disabling the communication channels from one cell to another. I think they were called gap channels or junctions or something."

Kody scratched the back of his head and leaned against the fence. Dane could see thoughts whirling inside that mind which would remain unknown to anyone but the thinker. And, though he was curious about what these ideas might be, he was content to simply be the catalyst for them.

He broke the contemplative silence. "Okay. Let's say all of this is true." He hit Kody's arm playfully. "You're bacteria, and I'm bacteria, and everything we do just leads toward the destruction of our planet and ourselves, right?" He leaned toward Kody. "So what? What are we supposed to do? Kill ourselves? Kill each other? I mean, with your logic"—he pointed at Kody—"those things wouldn't be tragedies. They'd be reducing the population, curing the infection."

After a short silence, Kody said, "I've thought about that." He nodded slowly. "There are times when I'll see a natural disaster on the news, and the death toll will be high, and I'll catch myself thinking, *Oh, good, that'll help.*"

Dane shook his head. "That's messed up, man."

"Is it?"

"Yes! Because no matter what you *think*, we're human. And we're here together. And every one of those dead people had a family and a life. They had feelings."

"Unless they were a sociopath."

Dane gestured toward Kody. "Like you."

Kody looked at the ground.

"I'm kidding, man. You wouldn't be able to write those songs if you couldn't relate to people." Dane stepped from the fence and turned around. "But that doesn't make your views on humanity any less messed up."

"Those aren't necessarily my views." Kody glanced sheepishly at Dane. "I'm not completely sold on what I just said. But I do think about those things—a lot." He indicated the van in the distance. "Driving around, all I do is think." Fidgeting in his pocket again. "I want to believe that there's some higher reason for us, that we're doing something positive by being here." Kody stared across the property. "But with all the horrible things going on in the world—with all the horrible things we're *doing* to the world, and to each other—I have trouble convincing myself that that's the case." After a long pause, he refocused on Dane. "What do you think about us, what we are?"

The pasture behind Kody rolled into darkness.

"I think we're all a part of something," Dane replied. "Something huge that we'll never understand." He pointed at Kody. "And, like you were saying, I believe we're all cells in some gigantic organism. 'The Everything' is what I call it." Dane slid his hands into the pockets of his shorts. "I don't think we're *cancer* cells, but I think we serve some purpose." He shrugged. "And I don't pretend to know what that is, but I do know what feels good. And, really, that's all I have to guide me. So I do that. I do what feels good and hope that I'm doing good for others in the process."

"That wouldn't work though," Kody hissed. "If everyone just did what felt good, there'd be nothing but robbery, and rape, and murder."

Dane noted the intensity in Kody's eyes. "You know, those things might feel good for some people." He looked across the field, toward the fire, where Risa threw her head back in laughter. "But I'm chasing different desires."

40

"You wrote that?" Deven asked, seated on a stump, face glowing with firelight.

Kody nodded and passed the guitar to Dane, lounging in a camping chair.

"Damn." Deven stood and offered the whiskey across the flames to Kody. "Heavy stuff."

Risa touched Dane's leg. "Play that new one you were talking about."

"It's not all the way finished." Dane scooted forward and positioned the guitar. "Actually, I was just messing around with one of the verses in my head. But I'll show you what I've got so far." After clearing his throat, Dane started to strum, and Kody pressed the bottle to his lips, curious how the violinist would handle a guitar.

Embers ascended into the blackness as Dane began to sing.

"I wanna stay forever, beneath Southwestern skies,

Where you and me lived wild and free, feelin' blessed to be alive.

I wanna stay forever, where the river's our backyard.

The campfire light dancing in your eyes, underneath a billion stars."

Risa scanned the sky while one leg, slung over the other, kicked to the rhythm.

"I wanna stay forever and breathe the cool, clean air.

Lifting veils, unraveling layers, until our souls are standing bare.

I wanna stay forever, on those rocks beside the creek.

Our skin well-done in the springtime sun, and we felt no need to speak."

Searching for flaws in Dane's writing and performance, Kody reluctantly concluded that the chords were well-chosen. Dane's lyrics evoked nostalgic imagery, and his voice was smooth and honest.

"Ooooh, ain't it magic.

While I'm swimming through those seas there in your eyes."

"Mmmm," Risa hummed softly, tapping a finger to the beat.

"Ooooh, yes, it's magic. When everything in life just lines up right. "

Deven smacked his hands together. "I'm feeling this one, for sure." He made a clicking noise and reached toward Kody. "Lemme get that bottle again."

Kody passed it over the flames, and a heated pressure began to boil in his depths. He reminded himself of Deven's positive response to his own song, and the temperature dropped, frenzied bubbles settling.

"Ooooh, ain't it magic."

Risa swayed like a charmed snake.

"While I'm swimming through those seas there in your eyes."

Deven tilted the bottle back, snapping along with his free hand.

"Ooooh, yes, it's magic. When everything in life just lines up right."

Erupting from his core, the Feeling rushed into Kody's limbs, barreling toward his extremities like scalding sludge. He imagined a metal door at the opening of each ear, thick and soundproof as that of a bank vault. Miniature men sprinted from his alarm-wailing brain—one up each auditory canal—and grabbed the handles of their respective doors. Leaning back with their entire body weights, they pulled the doors shut in tandem, blocking the catchy melody that pounded relentlessly upon the ego-shielding steel.

"Shit. One of your songs even made Risa cry."

In the cocoon of himself he'd created, the incessant thumping gradually faded to silence, and he admired the gleaming walls of his metallic space—slick and impenetrable, stainless and immaculate. Except for one small section, which appeared to have been etched by diamond or some other capable substance. A deafening thud echoed throughout the room, and Kody's heart dispatched adrenaline through his entire system in one violent command.

Pulse throbbing, he crept forward, focusing on the part of the wall in question. A single word was written in jagged font: *RED.*

"You say you're a songwriter as well?"

Kody wheeled around and saw himself, Red, and Dane seated on leather couches in the Nashville studio. Dane answered the producer's question. "I don't know if I'd call myself a *songwriter*, but I do write songs."

A warm smile washed across Red's lips. "I'd like to hear one, if you don't mind." He glanced at Kody and nodded toward an acoustic guitar on the wall. "Pass him that, will you?"

"Ooooh, ain't it magic."

The vault doors opened, and Dane's lazy strumming and meaningless lyrics rushed in. Metallic walls dissolved into the empty night, which hung above Risa and Deven like some endless, inky blob hung by tenuous strings, which, once cut, would allow it to finally crush everything it longed to smother below.

"While I'm swimming through those seas there in your eyes."

Risa and Deven's bodies sang unconscious praises for Dane as Kody peered over his shoulder at the lifeless pasture, wondering what creatures might be lurking in the darkness.

41

At two a.m., Risa parked her Subaru along the curb while Dane, in the passenger seat, checked his phone and took a sharp breath. "Here we go."

She glanced at him. "What?"

Dane held the phone up so Risa could see the screen, and her eyes glowed with anticipation as she squeezed his thigh. "Ooooh!"

With the phone's light illuminating his face, Dane read the message aloud. "'Dane. Thank you for the timely response. Your playing would be a perfect fit for these songs.'" His voice jumped an octave as his pace increased. "'Why don't you give me a call tomorrow? And we'll work out the details of the session!'"

Risa shook Dane's leg with both hands, yelling, "Whaaat?"

He turned and cupped Risa's cheeks. "No way!"

Grabbing his face, she released a smattering of kisses before running a hand through Dane's hair. She drew back to look at him. "I'm so excited for you."

Dane shook his head. "I can't believe it."

"You should believe it. You're great."

He smiled. "Thank you, *bonita*."

Blinking slowly, Risa emitted a soft, drawn-out hum. "I like when you call me that."

"Just reporting the truth."

"Cor-ny." She reached down and lifted her bag from the floor beside Dane's leg. "Let's go inside and celebrate."

"What time do you work?"

"Seven."

Dane slid the phone into his pocket. "You're a trooper. You know that?"

"I also have some really good coffee."

They exited the Subaru, and Risa locked it with her keychain while they started up the path to her apartment. From behind, a male voice shouted, "Hey!" and Risa gasped, whipping around. Vithu stood on the sidewalk, chest puffed, arms ready at his sides. He pointed at Dane. "Who the fuck is this?"

Risa dug a hand into her bag, and Dane stepped forward. "Hey, bud—"

Vithu closed the gap. "What?" He spoke inches from Dane's face. "You got something to say?"

A primal jolt electrified Dane, sharpening his senses, and he breathed from his stomach, steadying himself. *Stay focused,* he thought. *Just like last time.* "I think—"

Vithu sidestepped, pointing at Risa. "You're on your phone now?" He clenched a fist. "But you can't answer when *I* call?"

Risa spoke frantically, "Please. I need an officer to come to 1475 East—"

Vithu lunged toward Risa, but Dane shoved a hand into his chest.

"The fuck!" Vithu swatted Dane's hand away and swung wildly. As he stumbled with his own momentum, Dane shuffled to the side, imagining a target on Vithu's cheek. He cocked his fist and fired. The punch connected with a dull thud.

"No!" Risa rushed toward the fight.

Vithu fell, catching himself with his palms before reaching for Dane's leg, which lifted as Dane stepped away. Standing over Vithu, Risa yelled, "Get OUT of here!"

Dane grabbed her arm, yanking her back before positioning himself between her and Vithu, who rose to his feet.

Dane pointed up the street. "Leave. Now."

Vithu scowled and spit in Dane's face.

Dane jabbed, and Vithu ducked while punching him in the stomach. Doubling over, Dane choked out a guttural "Huuuh!" and clutched Vithu's collar, which ripped as Vithu wrapped his arms around Dane and attempted to kick his legs out from under him.

Hearing the commotion, two male neighbors rushed in and stepped between the fighters, prying them apart. One neighbor yelled, "Stop it!" over sirens screaming in the distance. Frantically, Vithu looked around, peering over one neighbor's shoulder and locking eyes with Dane, who steeled his gaze.

Risa's voice was chilling and fierce. "Vithu. Fucking GO!"

The sirens drew closer. Police lights flashed at the end of the block. Eyes alive with rage, Vithu glared at Risa before he turned and sprinted up the road.

42

Kody **woke to the crowing of roosters** and removed the sleep mask from his eyes, revealing the van's foggy windows. The smell of manure filled his nostrils as a horse huffed nearby. Kody slid the door open and stepped barefoot onto the wet grass, gazing up at a gray and gloomy sky. A thin mist hovered above the field like the ghost of the night prior.

Kody remembered the winery, the glass studio, the weed. He recalled the things he'd said to Dane and rubbed his forehead, exhaling heavily. Then he thought about the campfire, about Dane's song, and he knew what he had to do. Sitting on the running board and smoking a cigarette, Kody called Red. The phone rang twice before the producer answered, "Morning."

"Hey, Red."

"Your boy sent me some tracks. You're right. He's good."

Dane already contacted him.

"I was wondering." Kody took a drag. "Why don't you send me the names of those other fiddlers? I want to be sure Dane's the right one before moving forward."

"Oh, Kody. It may be too late for that. He called first thing this morning. As far as I knew, you were on board for having him, so I went ahead and locked him in, got him up to speed on things." Red took a sip of something. "He seems very enthusiastic about the project too, which is the kind of energy I like my players to have. It'd be a shame to turn back now." He paused. "On top of that, I think it'd be a good idea to bring him in considering the two of you have already played together."

Kody's jaw tightened as he contemplated challenging the producer's opinion.

Red continued, "I sent him the demos to play along with, and we kicked a few ideas back and forth."

I'll have to think of a different way to get Dane off the session.

"All right." Kody tapped the cigarette, ashes fell toward the grass. "I'm starting the drive tomorrow, so I'll see you in a couple days."

"Safe travels."

Kody hung up and peered through the pasture fence. The morning mist dissipated with a breeze that rustled the branches of a large willow. Beside the tree, a muscular mare grazed on her grassy breakfast.

A gate clicked, and Kody looked across the property where Deven, towel around his waist, padded toward a wooden shack from an outdoor shower enclosed by a five-foot-tall fence. Kody smothered the cigarette, ambled around to the back of the van, and opened the hatch. Out of his backpack, he fished fresh clothes and a towel. If he hurried, he could shower and leave before Deven could talk to him.

43

Before living on the road, Kody had worked in the warehouse of a musical-instrument store in Portland, Oregon. Every day was the same: he'd show up at eight in the morning, receive shipments, open boxes, stock the floor, call in repair orders, pack and ship outgoing items, and daydream about being anywhere but that soul-crushing hole.

Beyond cigarette breaks, the only part of the day he considered tolerable was a half-hour lunch that he could sometimes stretch to forty-five minutes. On his break, Kody would walk to the sandwich shop, buy a turkey sub, and eat it while returning to work. This process took about ten minutes. After the meal, he would grab an expensive guitar from the acoustic-instrument room and take it back to the warehouse.

A short door in the warehouse opened into a claustrophobic space with a low, slanted ceiling. The cave, as it was called, was where employees kept the overstock amplifiers. It was also the only place in the building where Kody could lose himself in a moment of uninterrupted song.

One afternoon, while returning to work—ducking through the cramped doorway with a guitar—he had an epiphany. The few minutes that he spent making music in the cave were the best of each day.

What if I was able to do that all the time?

In his head, Father's voice slurred an answer, "You wanna play songs for a living? Well, I wanna get paid to drink." Kody shook the idea, grabbed a clipboard, and headed to the sales floor to count microphone cables.

As the months wore on, Kody's life unfurled into one unbearably tedious routine. Music was his only source of relative contentment. In addition to his time in the cave, he would play obsessively before and after work, writing several songs per week. One evening at the store, he heard a saleswoman bragging about the money she'd made while street performing near the food trucks downtown. Two days later, aching for an experience that didn't involve packing tape, he drove to the outdoor food court, laid his open guitar bag on the sidewalk, and began to play.

The asphalt radiated summer heat as Kody sang timidly, his eyes shut behind sunglasses. Cars passed, people yapped, and planes roared overhead. To prevent the noise from drowning out his music, he strummed more forcefully and pushed his voice from his stomach, launching it purposefully toward the ears of meandering passersby. After three nerve-wracking minutes, the song ended to no applause. Tingling with adrenaline, he opened his eyes to see no audience except a couple pigeons on the sidewalk, and he concluded that street performing was a waste of time.

I should be practicing instead.

He bent to pick up his guitar bag, which, to his surprise, was littered with bills. Looking around, he noticed a white family seated on a nearby bench, watching expectantly.

"Good song," the dad said while chewing a bite of gyro.

Kody waved self-consciously. "Thanks."

"Yours?"

Kody nodded.

The dad stood and rummaged through his pocket as a chunk of onion fell from the gyro. "You don't have any CDs." He walked toward Kody. "Go buy some blank discs and get that recorded." The dad pitched twenty dollars into the guitar bag. "I wanna be able to listen to it in my car someday." He winked and walked back to his family.

Nodding gratefully, Kody decided to play one more song.

That single song turned into an afternoon of busking, cut short only because he broke a string and had neglected to bring replacements. After counting the cash he'd made that day, Kody decided he would play at the food trucks at least once a week from there on out, weather permitting.

On his fifth week of street performing, a man who booked talent for a local brewery dropped a card in Kody's bag. Apprehensive but curious, Kody emailed him that night to ask about the gig. When the man offered to pay in three hours what the warehouse paid for a full day, Kody's escape route became clear.

Over the next year, he built up a circuit of venues between Portland, Eugene, and Bend, even heading toward the Idaho border, hitting towns like Baker City and Pendleton. He played two to five gigs a week, and, not needing more than his modest material existence—shoebox apartment, used car, worn-out clothes— he saved much of the money he made from shows.

With a packed performance schedule, Kody was able to cut his warehouse sentence down to two days a week. He filled his free time with songwriting, booking gigs, and contemplating the fact that even though he was making most of his money playing music, he still felt a nagging discontentment. He began to dread playing the same songs night after night. He also became progressively annoyed at patrons who didn't pay attention to the music or express appreciation via tipping or applause. He began to feel that he might be better than the gigs he was playing, and he decided to try to get his music to someone who could take him to the next level.

That December, country artist Cal Walker released an album that received widespread critical acclaim. His rugged face was all over the magazines, and folks at Kody's gigs had begun to request that he play Cal's songs (one of which he begrudgingly learned). The producer who had worked on Cal's album was Red Smith, whom Kody had researched. Seeing Red's list of credentials, Kody believed recording with someone like him could give him an escape from the endless cycle of cover-song-loaded sets in chatty taverns.

Entertaining the possibility, he pictured the producer seated at a computer, opening an email containing one of Kody's songs. After pressing play, Red leaned back in his chair, lacing his fingers across his stomach and closing his eyes. When the singing began, Red scoffed and shook his head before stopping the song and deleting the message.

Kody's attempts to supplant this shameful scenario conjured Father's voice, "You think that hotshot wants anything to do with a whiny bitch like you?" But, as the weeks went on, and despite the possible rejection, Kody couldn't stop thinking about teaming up with the prestigious producer.

He decided to try.

One day, while Kody scribbled in his notebook between potato chips in the break room, one of the audio guys walked in and made his way to the refrigerator. "What's up?" the guy asked as he opened the door and pulled out a stained Tupperware bowl. After shutting the refrigerator, he dug a fork from his pocket and removed the lint.

Kody didn't respond, and the audio guy opened the grease-splattered microwave door before placing the Tupperware inside. "Writing some lyrics?" He closed the door and pressed the button.

Kody deemed this worthy of a reply. "No."

The audio guy turned and rested a hand on his hip. "Well, what *are* you doing then?"

Kody didn't bother to look up from the notebook. "I'm brainstorming some recording ideas."

The audio guy tapped a finger on his Recording Department name tag. "I know someone who could probably help with that."

Glancing at his coworker, Kody practiced his sarcasm. "Could you help me get some studio time with *Red Smith*?"

The audio guy pulled the phone from his pocket, and, after a few seconds, held the screen toward Kody. "Have you tried the 'Contact' tab on his website?"

After driving from Deven's ranch to Austin, Kody pulled the van into the parking lot of a deceased car wash, where the once-bright colors of a self-serve scrubbing bay had been faded by the southern sun. He navigated the cracked asphalt and parked near a decrepit fence in the rear of the lot. Glancing at his phone, Kody saw a text from Stanley.

No shower today? ;)

Kody responded, *No.* Then he called Dane.

"You're alive."

Kody's head throbbed. "You could call it that."

"Fun times last night, man. Glad you decided to come out." Dane paused. "Did you see Deven at all this morning?"

"No. Showered and left."

"Well, I know he had a good time too." Dane's voice jumped. "Oh! Gotta thank you for having me out at that gig. What a killer spot that was, right?"

"Yeah," Kody replied. "Hey, what are you doing today?"

"Not much, man. Risa's at the hospital, and I'm just tweaking that song a bit. Why? You wanna meet up?"

Kody peered through the windshield as a black bird landed on a coin-operated vacuum. "Yeah. Text me the address and I'll come over."

Kody's initial contact with Red consisted of him filling out a form on the producer's website. Once completed, the forms were sent to a manager, who sifted through the stack and forwarded to Red what was worthy of his time. Thinking his message would likely end up in the trash heap, Kody attached a few phone-recorded songs to the form and hit *Send*.

At least I tried.

Two weeks later, when Kody got an email from Red's manager, he thought he would be reading a harsh reprimand, lashing out at Kody for having the gall to send such steaming shit to a man of top-shelf talent. When the email expressed that Red would like to speak with Kody about a potential collaboration, he was stunned.

After several days of nervous dread, the phone call came. Of the few words Kody said, he stumbled over most of them. When the call was over, he was left contemplating a price tag that left him reeling but also gave him a financial goal to strive toward.

Two days later, he reached out to confirm the session.

With the studio time locked in, Kody went back to working in the warehouse six days a week and performing any night he could. As the months rolled by, his life became a blur of work, gigs, practice, and peanut-butter-and-honey sandwiches (sometimes with slices of banana). He began to feel like he was living the same week on repeat, and his mind went numb as he cruised through life on autopilot. Day and night, he focused solely on this Nashville recording session, which, at that point, was a year out.

When Kody pictured another twelve months of this treadmill existence, he wanted to strangle himself with a guitar string. He had dark circles beneath his eyes. He often dreamt about stocking shelves. To save money, he never went out, never did anything.

Late one night, Kody woke and went to the bathroom to take a piss. While tilting his head back, mid-stream, an idea entered his mind.

What if I didn't have to pay rent anymore?

Kody shook himself dry, flushed, and sat on the toilet. "I could get out of this place." He spoke to the dirty shower curtain. "Maybe I could trade the car for some old van and put a bed in it. Drive around and play gigs anywhere I want. No more warehouse."

"What about the recording money?" the curtain asked.

"If there's no rent, and I stay booked most nights of the week, I should be able to make what I need in time for the session." Kody thought about his bank account. "I'll just need to keep expenses to a minimum." He visualized morning rush-hour, counting political platitudes on bumper stickers through his cracked windshield. "But I might not make it through another year in Portland."

The dirty shower curtain replied, "Do it, then."

46

Kody parked his van along the curb in front of Risa's apartment and called Dane, who sauntered up the concrete path a minute later. As Kody stepped from the vehicle and came around the front bumper, Dane raised his chin in greeting. "Hey, bud!"

Kody nodded.

"Aren't you hot in that coat?" Dane asked. "It's, like, eighty degrees out."

Kody shook his head and fingered the object in his pocket. "I'm fine."

"Good call on the sunglasses." Dane gestured toward a red Taurus behind the van. "I'm gonna grab mine real quick." As Dane opened the passenger door and leaned inside, Kody took note of the vehicle and plate number.

Wearing aviators, Dane emerged from the car and ran a hand through his blond mess. "Much better." He pointed a thumb. "Let's go chill by the pool."

"Is there AC inside?"

Dane chuckled and indicated the long black coat. "I knew it was too toasty for that thing." He turned up the path, speaking over his shoulder. "Yeah. Risa's got it nice and cool in the apartment."

Kody followed, eyeing a shrub of Texas sage that bloomed with violet flowers.

"Talked to Red this morning." Dane opened the metal gate and held it.

Kody passed through. "I heard."

"Super down-to-earth guy." Dane closed the gate, leading the way.

"I want to talk about the session."

"Good idea." Dane stopped at an apartment with a *Starry Night* mat. "We should definitely work out the details." He wiped his feet, opened the door, and went inside. Kody followed, closed the door, and sat on the couch. Dane took a seat in the chair across the room and leaned forward, elbows on his knees. "What were you thinking?" Dane glanced toward the closet. "Should I grab my fiddle?"

"No." Kody lifted a foot and rested the ankle on his knee. After removing his sunglasses, he inspected his beat-up shoe. "I was watching you and Risa last night." He looked at Dane. "And the wheels started turning."

Dane reclined, sliding the aviators up to his forehead.

"I've never seen two people with a connection like yours," Kody added. "And I think it'd be a shame for you to leave it behind."

"Yeah, man," Dane replied. "She's a trip, isn't she?"

Dane had missed the point, and Kody plucked a hair from his coat. "Will it be hard to leave her?"

"It will." Dane paused. "But this thing with you is a huge opportunity. And I've gotta chase that. I mean ..." He glanced toward the window. "It's just wild how it all worked out, man." He looked at Kody. "Meeting Risa and coming down to Austin. And then I meet *you* and that leads to recording with Red Smith back in Nashville." Dane shrugged. "It's crazy. But like I was telling you last night, the Everything takes care of me." He pointed upward. "Always has. And I'll never understand why it works that way, but it does."

Kody nodded slowly. "What if you lose her?"

Dane rubbed the back of his head. "I've thought about that." He peered at the hardwood floor as if it were his teleprompter. "I really had zero expectations coming down here." He looked at Kody. "I thought Risa and I would probably hang out, hook up a few times, have some laughs, and then I'd be on my way back to Tennessee." He smirked. "But that's when it happens, right? When you least expect it. When it's natural."

Kody couldn't relate.

"What I'll probably do is head up to Nashville, do the session with you, then see where Risa and I stand after that." Dane leaned forward and clasped his hands together. "I've never thought about long-distance dating. And, honestly, I haven't been big on committed relationships for a while now. Just been doing my own thing and enjoying it. But I really think this is a connection worth exploring. So if it means we fly back and forth for a while, maybe we'll try that. Could be fun."

Kody ran a finger along the object in his coat. "There are some bike-taxis on Sixth Street, here in Austin."

Dane grinned. "Yup. I saw those. It would be easy money down here too. No hills!"

Kody nudged the idea along. "Well, you have Red's contact info. If you wanted to stay in Austin for a while, you could probably book a future session with him."

Dane shook his head. "No, man. I don't want to take the chance that I might miss out. I'd kick myself if I blew my only shot to record with a legend." He gestured toward Kody. "I dig your songs too. I think it'd be fun to throw down on them. Having the recordings would be a great reminder of this trip."

Kody considered telling Dane that he was going to find another fiddler, but news of this would get back to Red, and, considering the producer wanted Dane to play, Kody couldn't risk upsetting Red this close to the session. After releasing a surrendering breath, Kody glanced at a picture of Risa on the wall behind Dane. She stood with an arm around a woman who looked like a version of her from the future. The blood-red sun sank into the ocean behind them.

Dane turned his head to see where Kody's attention was focused. "Isn't it crazy how much she looks like her mom?"

"Yeah." Kody shifted his gaze to another photo, where Risa's arms were raised above her head as though she were submitting to something inevitable and overpowering. Her smile was white-toothed and beaming, and behind her was a red rock formation that looked like a Martian cathedral. Parked down the road from Risa, nearly out of frame, was a modest RV with a few people around it. Kody glanced curiously at Dane. "Where have you been parking your RV?"

Dane pointed a thumb toward the window. "This little lot out in Dripping Springs. Haven't been spending any time in the rig 'cuz I've been staying here, but it's there if I need it."

Kody fingered the object in his pocket. "Which lot?"

47

Seated at the nurse's station, Risa read the doctor's decision via text: *digital disimpaction.*

She stood and released a heavy sigh. After grabbing pain medication, gloves, and a paper cup filled with water, she headed to room 405 where the eighty-two-year-old Mr. Nichols lay in his hospital gown, watching a game show.

"Hi, Mr. Nichols." Risa set the supplies on the counter and walked toward the sink.

Mr. Nichols turned his head and squinted with tired eyes, smiling feebly. "The angel returns."

Washing her hands, Risa made a low, contented sound and said, "How are you feeling?"

Mr. Nichols spoke in a labored voice, "My asshole. It hurts."

Caught off guard, Risa did her best to stifle a giggle as she turned the faucet off and dried her hands. "Well, I'm gonna give you something that will get us closer to stopping the hurt." She walked over to the counter, slid the gloves on, and grabbed the packaged pill and paper cup.

"Oh, that sounds nice," Mr. Nichols said dreamily.

Risa pulled a rolling table to the side of the bed and set the packaged pill on it. She held the paper cup in front of Mr. Nichols's mouth. "Let's take a sip."

Mr. Nichols leaned forward, pursed his dry lips, and took an eager slurp, coughing as he swallowed.

Risa withdrew the cup. "Oh!"

Mr. Nichols looked at her and raised a weak arm. "Got a tad excited."

"Yeah, you did." Risa set the cup on the table and opened the package. "Okay." She lifted the pill and cup and turned to him. "For real this time."

Mr. Nichols stuck out his tongue, and Risa administered the dose before holding the cup to Mr. Nichols's lips. After a drink, he swallowed and proudly opened his pill-free mouth.

"Good job." Risa put the used wrapper inside the paper cup. "Now, I'll be back in a minute, and we'll make that pain go away."

"Are you aware that a minute is sixty seconds?"

Risa smiled, knowing she often took longer than this to return. "I am."

"I'm holding you to it this time!" Mr. Nichols pointed a shaking finger and began to count, accenting each number with a nod that jiggled loose skin. "One. Two. Three. Four." As Risa left the room, the counting became quieter. "Nine. Ten. Eleven." When she reached the nurse's station, Kylie, another day-shifter, looked at her and said, "Having fun in there?"

"You busy?"

Kylie peeked past Risa, into Mr. Nichols's room. "I don't know. Why?"

"I could use some backup."

Smirking, Kylie tapped a pen against her cheek. "What for?"

With one hand, Risa made a sideways fist. With the other, she used a finger to slowly penetrate it. "Digital disimpaction."

Kylie dropped the pen onto the desk and feigned a gag. "Okay, but he's your patient, so I'm rolling him while you poke."

"Lucky us, right?" Risa leaned onto the counter. "Can you think of any other job where you'd say something like that? 'I'll roll him while you poke'"

Kylie stood, and an impish grin lifted her cheeks. "Maybe a couple." She came around to the other side of the desk. "I'm gonna go to the bathroom real quick."

As she left, Risa heard a yell from a nearby room.

"No! Don't pull on that." She recognized the voice as Gabby's. "Mrs. Lee, I know it's uncomfortable, but I'm gonna need you to leave that tube alone."

Turning around to lean against the nurse's station, Risa shook her head and allowed herself a moment of full sensory presence. Somewhere between the stifling, sterile odor and the retina-raking glow of fluorescent light—the reflection of which gleamed atop the polished linoleum—Risa imagined her future. She pictured her career two decades from now, after all the traveling had been done and the excitement had worn thin, seeing herself like so many of the lifers she'd met over the years—jaded, callous, and complaining of back pain.

"Mrs. Lee, please! That catheter needs to stay in."

Risa glanced toward the restrooms. No sign of Kylie. She went around the nurse's station and dug into the pocket of her coat, draped across the back of an office chair. Sitting down, she opened a social media app and began to scroll past photos of newborn babies and perfectly plated food, searching for distraction from thoughts of a monotonous future. She tapped on the profile of a mural artist she followed, and a tinge of jealousy accompanied the girl's latest post.

Bonnie, two years younger than Risa, sat on a stool atop a paint-splattered sheet in the middle of a hardwood-floored room. Propped against the sunlit walls were four canvases, taller than the artist, alive with bold colors and twisting shapes. The caption read, *Finally finished these giant paintings for a science-research building in San Diego and am delivering them tomorrow! Next stop: Mexico City for a month-long mural project!*

Risa sifted through Bonnie's prior posts: a poolside wall in LA decorated with a rainbowed rendition of the Hollywood sign, in front of which several iconic celebrities had been painted striking their signature poses; an elevator in

Bali transformed into a fiery sunset scene, its reds and oranges made even more vibrant in contrast to the silhouetted palm trees looming in the foreground. Then there was Bonnie relaxing on some white sand beach with an umbrella cocktail in hand. *Just another day at the office :)*

"You ready?" Kylie stood over Risa, pulling on her gloves.

Risa sighed and closed the app. "I guess."

48

After passing a towering church, Kody turned off the highway and drove along a road that dipped and rose again like an asphalt roller coaster, revealing a winding route through the brush-studded hills of Dripping Springs. The navigation app said the destination was on the left, so Kody slowed the van and turned into the semicircular gravel path that wound around an island of oak and elm. The first camp spot was occupied by a large motorhome; the next was taken by a sea-green VW van; two spaces after that was a sedan with a tent pitched nearby. The van rolled along until Kody came to a small RV with Tennessee plates. A tow dolly rested near the water hookup. Slowing to a stop, he surveyed the area. Parked one space over, and mostly blocked from view by two expansive trees, was a diesel pickup with a large camper. No one occupied the site on the other side of Dane's RV.

Kody checked his phone: 4:36. Sunset would be just after 8:00.

After exiting the lot, he drove along the narrow, twisting road to search for a place where he could nap until darkness. Navigating a tight curve, Dane's song popped into his head.

Ooooh, ain't it magic.

Kody ran a hand through his hair and began to hum one of his own tunes. The road bent left. Several curious houses peered down from the hillside. Ahead was a pickup with a bed full of landscaping equipment. Kody's breathing accelerated. Each expansion of the lungs burned as if he were inhaling weed killer. To distract himself, he sprayed wiper fluid and activated the blades. Dead bugs smeared across the glass. On the left was a dirt driveway leading to an open plot of land. Kody veered onto the gravel shoulder and checked the side mirror before making a U-turn and driving back to the lot. After pulling in, he assessed the vegetation-lined perimeter. Other than a large pile of branches and limbs on the far side, the area was clear. The van rocked from side to side as he drove over the uneven dirt, headed toward the debris.

Once parked, Kody silenced the engine, leaving rapid-fire thoughts to bombard his consciousness. He reached beneath the seat, grabbed his flask, and took a long pull. The whiskey clawed his esophagus, all the way down. After a second sip, Kody felt only a muted ache behind his eyes where the thoughts had been. Clutching the steel container, he stared through the windshield, allowing himself to become mesmerized by the branches and leaves swaying in the breeze. One more gulp, and he screwed the cap on before stashing the flask beneath the seat.

He opened the door, stepped out, and slid the back door wide. After kicking his shoes onto the dirt, he crawled onto the mattress and closed the slider. Then he shut the curtains and pulled a pillow from beside the bed frame. "Too hot for a blanket." He wrestled his coat off and positioned the pillow beneath his head. Turning sideways, he drew a long breath and released a groan until every bit of air had been pushed from his lungs. He did this several times, picturing himself as a deflating balloon, and his head grew gradually lighter. As the muscles around his ribcage began to slacken, the tingling in his chest rippled into his fingers. Outside, a propeller plane buzzed overhead, carrying on until its lonesome sound disappeared.

49

Seated at the recording console, Red pressed the button that enabled him to talk to the drummer in the live room. "Let's hear that kick drum."

There was a muffled "Gotcha" from the studio monitors, followed by a series of deliberate thumps. Dane sat on a stool in the corner of the room, casually strumming a vintage acoustic guitar and humming a melody while surveying the space.

"Dane." Red glanced over his shoulder.

"Sorry, man." Dane set the guitar on the stand beside him. "It's such a sexy Gibson. I had to try it out."

Red grinned. "You're fine." He nodded toward the guitar. "What were you playing?"

The kick drum went *thump, thump, thump* as Kody glared from his seat on the other side of the room.

"This new tune I've been working on," Dane replied.

Kody opened his mouth to speak, but no sound came.

Red pressed the button. "Hold on." The kick stopped, and Red spun in his chair, pointing at the guitar. "Play it again."

Kody stood and strode across the room, where he attempted to snatch the guitar, but his fingers passed through the neck as though he were an apparition. "This is *my* session!"

Oblivious to Kody, Dane lifted the Gibson and began to play while Red rubbed his chin, nodding thoughtfully. As Dane started to sing, Kody swung, but the punch was halted an inch from Dane's head by some invisible force. The room darkened, and the edges of Kody's vision faded to nothing. He turned, inhaling sharply.

There was no studio, only blackness.

Wheeling around, Kody saw that Dane and Red had vanished. In their places stood tall firs rooted in moss-covered dirt. Rain drizzled from the gray sky. Kody's hands were hot, and he inspected his palms to find them streaked with blood. He opened his mouth to scream, but no sound came. Dropping to his knees, he rubbed his hands maniacally through the mud, running them back and forth until the blood was his.

Kody woke in the van. Darkness outside. Except for his frantic heartbeat—*thump, thump, thump*—there was silence.

Now.

He slid the curtain aside, opened the door, and sat on the running board.

After dusting rocks from his socks, he pulled his shoes on. Then he slid into his coat, closed the door, and went around to the back of the van. Once the tailgate was open, he grabbed an L-shaped tire iron from beside the bed frame and closed the hatch. He walked to the driver's door, climbed inside, and drove in reverse before putting it in gear to exit the lot.

The van sped up the road, winding between hateful hills. The impressive church loomed ahead like a castle housing some world-burning spirit. Kody turned into the church's empty lot and drove to the back corner, where he parked and killed the engine. He grabbed the tire iron and climbed out. Beneath the moon—hanging like a scythe blade—Kody took quick, deliberate steps. He marched up the road. No headlights in sight. Moving briskly, he glanced over his shoulder.

No headlights behind.

The campground was quiet except for Kody's shoes crunching across the gravel and the muffled barking of a dog. He noticed a light on in the camper at the next site. Moving stealthily, Kody approached Dane's RV and raised the tire iron. The first strike landed with a glassy smack, leaving a spiderweb crack in the middle of the windshield. Kody grunted and drew the weapon back, slamming it down repeatedly, each blow more violent than the last. Cracks and dents intersected with one another like some horrible mandala, and Kody's muscles burned as he swung over and over. Behind him, the camper door flung open, hitting the side of the trailer with a thud and throwing light across the RV's windshield. For a moment, Kody saw beauty in the twinkling cracks that split jaggedly across the glass. The dog's barking grew louder, more menacing, and Kody turned as a man in a trucker hat shouted, "Ay!"

Kody ran. The barking followed. After exiting the campground and whipping right, Kody bolted up the road.

In the distance, the man yelled, "Stop!"

Legs aching, arms pumping, Kody peeked over his shoulder. A gray pit bull was gaining on him. The church towered ahead, and he ran toward it as fast as he could, breathing heat, growing dizzy. Headlights appeared on the road, and he ducked into the brush, darting between sage, leaping over branches. A rock caught his foot, sending him sprawling across the dirt. The tire iron flew from his hand and landed with a hollow smack. He flipped onto his back, hearing a snarling growl and the patter of determined paws. Kody thrust a hand into his coat pocket as the dog sped closer. He felt for the object, found it, pulled it out.

The blade glinted in the moonlight.

V

No Return

50

"What did you guys do?" Risa lay naked beneath the comforter, her hair fanned across the pillow.

"Just hung out for a while, shot the shit." Dane, also naked, rinsed his toothbrush and set it on the bathroom counter. As he padded toward Risa, she amused herself by concluding that the extreme contrast of his tan lines made his legs look like he'd waded through knee-high mud. "We talked about recording, threw a few ideas around. He's leaving in the morning, so we'll end up working out the details when I get to Nashville." Dane climbed into bed, where Risa lifted herself so Dane could slide an arm beneath her.

"I don't know how to feel about Kody," Risa said, facing Dane.

"He's a tough one to read, but I think he's coming around. We had a pretty long talk last night."

"Do you like him?"

Dane looked at her. "Honestly, if it wasn't for this recording session, or his music, I don't think I'd be hanging with the guy. He's pretty uptight." He paused, catching his thoughts. "I mean ... I guess he'd be all right to sit and have a few drinks with. If I was in the mood to talk about deep stuff, he'd be good for that."

Risa thought about Kody's eyes, remembering their penetrating hunger. "There's some darkness in him."

Dane chuckled. "Way to be dramatic." He gently pinched her nipple. "Not every guy is Vithu, you know."

"I mean it." She pushed his hand away and propped herself up on an elbow. "I get this nasty feeling about him."

"I was a little put-off by him at first too." Dane laced his fingers behind his head. "But I think that's just how he is—really serious, kinda comes off as an asshole."

Risa rolled onto her stomach and rested her chin atop folded arms. "I'm talking about something *else* though." She looked at Dane, wondering if she was being too judgmental, or maybe he was too naive. "Something I can't explain, but I feel."

"Okay, check this out." Dane turned onto his side, supporting his head with one hand. "One of the things Kody said today was that you and I had a palpable chemistry. He asked how I felt about going back to Nashville, and he even offered to find someone else to do the session if I wanted to spend more time down here with you."

Risa's stomach fluttered.

"Does that sound like *darkness* to you?" he asked.

Risa forfeited her attempt to combat Dane's optimism. "What did you say when he asked you that?"

Dane rubbed a thumb across Risa's cheek. "I told him leaving will be tough." He scanned her eyes. "That the last few days have been paradise."

"Mmmm." Risa grew a soft smile. "They have." She glanced at the comforter before looking at Dane. "So what do we do now?"

Dane rolled onto his back. "I've been thinking about that." He stared at the ceiling as if the answer were etched there. "I didn't know what to expect coming down here. I didn't expect anything, really."

"Setting the bar low."

"Well." Dane grinned, looking at her. "I knew we'd have a good time, 'cause we had a great connection in Nashville. But I wasn't sure what was gonna happen beyond that. I mean, I could have come down to find out you were a heroin addict or a Mormon or something."

Risa laughed. "How can you compare those?"

Dane winked. "Like I told you, I haven't been in a relationship for a while. And it's been good, flying solo." He caressed Risa's arm. "But I wouldn't be able to go back to Tennessee and not think about you. It'd be impossible." He shook his head. "And if I didn't put some energy into staying connected with you, I'd never stop wondering what would have happened if I had."

Risa bit her lip as a tsunami of relief whisked her away. "That makes me happy."

"Yeah?"

She nodded.

"Good, 'cuz I wasn't sure where you were at with all of this. And being on the same page makes lying naked together a lot less awkward."

Risa thrust a hand forward to tickle Dane's torso, and he swatted it away. When she tried again, he grabbed her wrist and pinned it against the mattress. She used her other hand, but he pinned that one too, saying, "You're in a pretty compromising position now, aren't you?"

Risa kicked her feet wildly and squeaked while scrunching her face with eyes shut.

"Hey," Dane said through a grin.

Risa stopped kicking and looked at him.

He leaned in. "Come here."

She scooted closer and brought her mouth to his, parting her lips, feeling the heat, losing herself in a moment she wished would last forever.

Kody was startled awake by the rumble of a large engine. Headlights flooded the back of the van, and he sat up, shielding his eyes from the glare as two doors shut in succession and a pair of male voices slurred drunkenly. Something thumped against the van.

"Hey, mailman!" one of the men called out. "I got a p-package for you."

"You ain't got shit," the other taunted.

"Like hell, I don't."

Kody flinched as he heard another thump on the van.

"Here, gimme a hand," the first man said.

The van began to rock back and forth. "Wakey, wakey!"

Kody lifted the pillow and shifted his knife into position beneath the blanket. He opened the curtain. "Whoa!" One of the men jumped back as Kody slid the door open. The Texas night was warm and quiet. Behind the men, a corn silo stood like a silver sentinel guarding endless rows of crop.

"Hey," one man said, pointing at Kody. "You ain't no mailman."

"No."

The other man stepped forward, his breath reeking of booze. "What're you doin' parked on my daddy's land?"

"Drove from Austin tonight. Headed to Nashville." Kody analyzed every facial nuance, every slight movement. "Almost fell asleep on the highway."

Without acknowledging that he'd heard Kody, one of the men reached into the van to feel the metal grating that covered the window. "What's this cage for?" he slurred. "You got a' animal or somethin'?"

Beneath the blanket, Kody's hand inched forward. "I am the animal."

The man laughed, spraying spit.

Kody wished the man had seen him earlier with the tire iron, the dog.

Eyes glazed, the guy stared at Kody and slowly withdrew his arm, swaying involuntarily.

Kody stared back, wrangling his breathing, running a finger along the blade.

"Let's scoot." The other man took a sip of his beer and tipped the can toward Kody. "Hey, animal."

Kody looked at him.

"Nap's over. You got five minutes to get out."

52

Beneath a clear and placid sky, Risa and Dane ambled along the concrete path that led from her apartment to the street. Once they'd reached the sidewalk, Dane, clutching the straps of his backpack, looked at her and said, "All right, *bonita*. I'll call you tonight when I set up camp in Arkansas."

They stopped walking, and Risa poked a bulging vein in Dane's forearm. "I wish I could come with you." Gazing into his eyes, she shifted her shoulders back and forth like a child hiding a secret. "My turn then?"

"For what? Visiting?"

Risa nodded.

"Sounds good. Maybe we can even hit Memphis for a few days."

"Ooooh." She folded her hands beneath her chin. "Yes, please."

Dane chuckled and patted Risa's butt through her cerulean skirt. "Oh!" He held up a finger. "Hold on." He slung his backpack off one shoulder, bringing the bag around his chest and unzipping the main compartment to reach inside.

What's he up to?

After rummaging through the pack, Dane handed Risa a small cardboard box. "What's this?"

He nodded toward the gift. "Open it."

Risa's pulse hastened as she turned the box around, searching for a way inside. The contents were too weighty to be jewelry, and no discernable scent emanated from the folds. A small, pencil-shaped icon adorned one corner.

"Here." Dane presented his keys, which she used to cut the Scotch tape that held the box shut.

Risa lifted the lid, revealing hundreds of tiny cards stuffed inside. Curiously, she glanced at Dane, whose eyes glowed with anticipation. "Take one out," he urged.

Using her thumb, she slid the first card upward and was surprised to see herself smiling back. *Why is my profile picture on here?* Reading the text beside the photo, she gasped. *Risa Morales. Painter.* Beneath this title, typed in bold, was her email and phone number, as well as social media links.

A wave of warmth swept through her, and she looked up at Dane. "But ... I'm not—"

"Look," he said. "You don't have to do anything with these, but maybe you could just carry a few business cards around in your wallet, look at them every now and then." He zippered the pack and returned it to his back. "Who knows? If you see your name next to 'painter' a few times, maybe you'll begin to see your art the same way I do."

She looked at him, and the warmth intensified, heating her cheeks. "This might be the sweetest thing anyone has done for me." She wrapped her arms around Dane, squeezing hard, careful not to dump the box's contents onto the pavement. After a long embrace, she stepped back and turned the card over, shocked to see a painting she'd done of flowers on a West Virginia hillside. "How did you—"

"Took a picture of it when you weren't looking." Dane beamed with pride.

"You didn't."

He nodded.

Risa sighed, examining both sides of the card. "Well, I have to say, it looks really nice on here."

"It's a beautiful piece." Dane rubbed her shoulder. "It'd look good even if it was painted on the side of a Porta-Potty."

Risa threw him an amused glance. "Way to ruin the moment."

"I've gotta say one more thing."

She cocked her head.

"I swear it's serious."

Risa arched a skeptical eyebrow.

"I started playing the violin in elementary school," Dane began. "My stepdad wanted me to get into it—something about connecting with my Scandinavian roots. I was resistant at first, but as I started to get comfortable with the instrument over the years, I'd catch myself rushing home after school so I could sit in my room and play for hours.

"I'd pick rock bands I liked—Green Day or Nirvana, stuff like that—and I'd try to turn the vocal or guitar melody into a fiddle part. Once I got good at that, I began to improvise solos over the instrumental sections of the song. Then I started to write my own music."

"And now you're going to record in Nashville."

Dane's dimples appeared on either side of his grin. "I guess what I want to say is, I was always very shy about playing in front of people." He crossed his arms. "I loved doing it in my room, by myself. Music was *my* meditation like painting is yours."

Risa imagined a teenaged Dane rocking out alone in his room. *Adorable.*

"One Summer afternoon, my older brother came into the room in the middle of me working on a song and he said, 'Come with me. Bring the violin.'" Dane beckoned with a finger, imitating his brother. "I tried to stay home, but he wouldn't take no for an answer. So I tried asking him where we were going, but he wouldn't tell me. Just said, 'Trust me. You'll have fun.'"

Dane shook his head. "I was terrified at first, when we walked toward his group of friends, all hanging out, sitting on a cliff above the ocean. They were the cool kids in high school, a few grades older than me. I was one of the skaters."

"What do you mean? Like roller skates?"

"Skateboarders." He formed the rock-and-roll sign with his hand. "We were the punks, the troublemakers." His smirk spread slowly. "We knew how to have fun."

Risa nudged him with her shoulder. "Not much has changed."

Dane took an exaggerated bow. "Pleasure to be of service." After straightening his posture, he continued, "Anyway, when we got up to the group, one of my brother's friends, Jean Marc, stood up and started talking about how he'd heard so much about my playing from Beau."

"Beau's your brother?"

Dane nodded. "Yeah. Turns out Beau had been bragging to everyone about me, and Jean Marc had brought his guitar to the bluff, hoping to jam with me."

"So ... Did you?"

"Not at first." Dane leaned in, lowering his voice. "Like I said, I was super shy." His confidence returned. "But all of us hung out for a while, and the group kept bugging me to play. On top of that, one of the girls there gave me some beers. I'd only had a few in my life up to that point, so they loosened me up pretty good."

"So *then* you played?"

"Yep."

"And?"

Dane stared into the distance, reliving the moment. "They loved it." He looked at Risa. "Jean Marc and I did, like, ten songs. A lot of covers that everyone knew, so they were all singing along and swaying to the music while the sun went down." Dane took one of Risa's hands, looking into her eyes. "My point is, that one moment, that little bit of encouragement from Beau, it changed my whole life. It was so powerful." He released her hand and indicated the business cards. "I'm not saying this is that moment for you, but if I can give you something similar to the push my brother gave me ..."

Risa waited for Dane to finish his thought.

"I don't know. I just think it'd be cool if you're able to see what I see when I look at your art." He ran a hand through his hair. "I think it's amazing."

Risa moved closer. "And *I* think you're a smooch."

Dane huffed a chuckle. "A what?"

"A smooch." She grabbed his T-shirt, gently pulling him toward her. "It means I really, *really* like you."

A flood of thoughts filled Risa's head as she closed her eyes and pressed her lips to Dane's. He was leaving for Nashville. *This might be our last kiss.* He had said they would see each other again. *But that's what they all say.* She told herself not to get her hopes up. *But there's something different about this time.* Finally, she managed to quiet the voices and enjoy the intensity of their focused passion, their feedback loop of human electricity—that funky thing he did with his tongue.

When she finally pulled back, Risa opened her eyes and released a low hum that buzzed in her chest, the sound that grounded her in moments when the goodness of life filled her to the brim. When she felt like a teakettle bursting with love and hope.

Allowing her gaze to drift, she glanced at the street behind Dane, where his red Taurus appeared to be parked oddly, leaning to one side. Inspecting the vehicle more closely, she gasped. "Oh my god."

Dane glanced curiously at Risa before turning and seeing the slashed tires. "Fuck."

Risa put both hands on top of her head. "I can't believe that psycho!"

Dane rubbed his chin and looked at her. "Who? Vithu?"

Marching toward Dane's car, Risa shot a look over her shoulder that said, *Of course.*

"You really think he'd take it this far?" he asked.

Risa whipped around and threw her arms up. "I'm sorry. Were you not in the car when he *chased* us?"

Dane scratched his head. "Right." He glanced at the sky. "Why is it always when I have a deadline that something like this happens?" Risa crouched beside one of the lacerated tires as Dane circled the car and said, "At least he only got the curb-side ones."

Risa ran a finger along the thick, chalky rubber inside the knife mark. "I can't believe it." She stood and looked at Dane, feeling like their perfect moment had been shattered. "I'm so sorry I got you into this."

Dane pulled the phone from his pocket and stroked a hand along Risa's arm. "Don't be sorry." He typed something into the phone. "You can't control the guy."

"Yeah, but I—"

"Hey." Dane held the screen out for her to see. "Down for a quick field trip?"

Hypnotized by the spinning clothes, Kody stared into the groaning machine. Two chairs away, a thin white woman in sandals, sweatpants, and a tank top was picking her nose while scrolling mindlessly on her phone. Kody fished his own phone from the pocket of his shorts.

No messages.

He hasn't seen it yet.

Kody rested the phone on the chair beside him and planned his impending conversation with Dane, then the one with Red.

A machine beeped, and a wide man pushed himself up from his chair on the other side of the room. As Kody watched him roll a laundry basket across the linoleum, scenes from the previous night flashed through his mind—the windshield, the tire iron, the catharsis—how satisfying it had felt to destroy. He remembered the man in the camper. Then he hated himself for turning to look.

How stupid.

After torturing himself by imagining scenarios where he did things properly, Kody pictured sprinting away from the scene, the dog charging after him. He glanced toward the dryer, hoping the extra-strength detergent had done its job.

He recalled driving into Austin, seeing the twinkling lights of downtown and the building that looked like a massive glass owl. He savored the fact that he'd been covert, how he had parked down the street from Risa's and stalked in the shadows. He remembered how easily the blade had penetrated the rubber and how quickly he had run back to the van.

As the tumbling clothes slowed to a stop, the dryer beeped. On the digital display, a red light flashed as Kody crossed the tile and opened the door. Digging through the socks, shirts, pants, and underwear, he found the long black coat and pulled it from the mix. Holding it up, he turned it around, inspecting it closely. As far as he could see, the blood was gone.

"The guy told me it would be around here," Dane said as he and Risa walked a dusty path between rows of cars, trucks, vans, and SUVs—vehicles of every make, model, and color. The best-looking doors had been scavenged. Several dent-free hoods and intact windows had been removed. Many scratchless bumpers were missing. Most of the tires had already been salvaged, leaving the majority of the vehicles resting on worn rims and rusty wheels.

Risa pointed to a green Taurus. "That one looks like yours."

Dane glanced at the vehicle, then at her. "Good eye." As they walked toward the car, he evaluated the tires. "They're in decent shape."

Farther down the line of deteriorating vehicles, two Mexican men were using a loud drill to remove the lug nuts from the wheel of a VW hatchback. Behind the men, a large cart was stacked with tires.

Dane and Risa circled the Taurus. "I think the back ones are the best looking." He opened the driver's door, leaned inside, and popped the trunk while Risa went around to open it. As Dane walked to the back, Risa pulled a jack from beneath the carpet. "No tire iron?" he asked. Risa shook her head, and Dane glanced at the Geo Prizm behind them. He walked over, leaned in through the missing driver's side window, popped the lever, and went around back, where he opened the trunk and dug through a layer of old magazines that disintegrated like dry autumn leaves. Beneath the mess lay a rusty tire iron. "Got one."

He went to the Taurus, removed the spare tire from the trunk, and tossed it onto the dirt, where it landed with a puff of dust.

"Hey," Risa called out to him. When Dane turned around, she planted a swift kiss on his cheek and handed him the jack before skipping to the Prizm, where she lay on the hood and closed her eyes to bask in the sun.

Effortless beauty, he thought.

Focusing on the task at hand, Dane knelt, setting the jack on the ground, and positioned the tire iron over one of the lug nuts. With all his strength, he pushed downward, leaning onto the bar, but the nut wouldn't budge. After several unsuccessful attempts to loosen it, Dane stood and stomped on the bar, which shifted slightly but still wasn't cooperating.

Hearing Dane's frustrated grunts, Risa opened her eyes and propped herself up. As she watched him struggle with the tire iron—hitting the bar with a rock he'd found lying nearby—she snickered, and the buzzing drill caught her attention. Glancing down the line, she stood and made her way toward the sound. A minute later, she returned with one of the tire-gathering men, who was clutching the large drill.

Wiping sweat from his forehead, Dane looked up at Risa, who grinned proudly as Dane scooted aside and said, "Thanks," to the man, who used the drill to loosen five lug nuts in rapid succession. The man stood and said something to Risa in fast-forward Spanish while circling around to the other side. Risa laughed and replied enthusiastically as Dane slid the jack beneath the car, wishing he'd paid more attention in señora Scott's class.

Once the man had loosened all the nuts, Risa said, "*Gracias!*"

The man smiled modestly and nodded before walking away.

Returning to her seat on the hood of the Prizm, Risa watched as Dane cranked the jack and raised the vehicle. He twisted the nuts loose and stored them in the pocket of his shorts. "That was a great idea," he said, grabbing the tire with both hands and yanking it from the wheel.

"That's his son over there." Risa peered down the line of cars. "They take those tires and sell them."

"Awesome way to bond." Dane laid the tire on the ground.

"Hmmm." Risa nodded to herself. "I think they're doing it more out of necessity, but the bonding is an added bonus."

Dane stood and scanned the yard, using a hand to shield his eyes from the sun.

"What are you looking for?"

"A rim."

Risa dusted the back of her long skirt and began to wander between vehicles, searching the ground.

"Or another tire!" Dane called out.

"Gotcha!"

Dane dropped to push-up position and peered beneath an SUV. As he searched the dirt for an object that would serve his purpose, he realized this would be the last morning he'd spend with Risa—*hopefully not ever, but at least for a while.* He wished she could come with him to Nashville, and he pictured the two of them on the road together, trading stories and stopping along the way to explore whatever side-quest caught their attention.

Sandaled feet crunched across the ground and a shadow fell over him. "Will this work?"

Dane appraised the large aluminum rim in Risa's hands. "That's perfect." He stood and took it as she dusted her palms. "Hey."

Risa glanced at him, and, after a long moment, a sheepish grin spread across her face. "What?"

He shook his head. "Just looking."

"You're a dork."

Kneeling behind the Taurus's back bumper, Dane slid the rim vertically beneath the center of it. He went to the side of the car and loosened the jack, lowering the back bumper onto the upright rim, which held the vehicle evenly suspended, rather than allowing it to lean toward its tireless side.

"Fancy," Risa said.

"Right?" Dane moved to the other side of the Taurus, pulled the tire off, and set it on the ground. After wiping his brow with a forearm, he tossed the jack into the trunk. "One more thing." Leaning in through the driver's side door, he popped the hood.

As Dane went to the front of the vehicle, Risa stood one of the tires up and rolled it to the dirt path.

Digging around beneath the hood, Dane plucked several fuses from the box and slid them into his pocket. "Never know when you may need a few of these."

Holding her tire upright, Risa nodded toward an old Pontiac. "Why don't you snatch that crusty air freshener too?"

Dane grinned and walked toward the back of the car, where he bent down, stood the other tire up, and rolled it toward the dirt path. "Oh, hold on." He leaned the tire against the car and jogged to the spot behind the trunk, where he lifted the spare from the ground, and, strutting toward Risa, said, "Lost my other one," as he used his free hand to roll the upright tire.

"Maybe this all happened for a reason then."

Dane searched Risa's face, radiant in the Texas sun. "Maybe."

Side by side, they rolled their rubber donuts up the dirt path. With a grunt, Risa pushed her tire ahead and ran to stabilize it before it fell over. Glancing over her shoulder, she waited for Dane to catch up. When he did, they rolled past a Volvo with the hood propped open and guts strewn about. Atop the antenna was a sun-blanched smiley-face ball that bobbed in the breeze—moving to the roaring soundtrack of the nearby highway, interrupted intermittently by the mechanized zip of a drill.

Risa lifted the dumpster lid while Dane used both hands to hurl one of the damaged tires over the rim. "Do you think we should call the police?" she asked.

"We can't prove it was Vithu." Dane picked up the other tire and tossed it into the dumpster. "I mean—he had a motive, but that's not enough for the cops to do anything about it."

"What if he *did* do it, though?" Risa let the lid fall with a thud.

"If he did, this might have been just what he needed to feel like the winner." Dane shrugged. "Maybe he'll leave you alone now." He wiped his palms on his shorts. "Has he called you?"

Risa shook her head. "Not since the night you punched him."

He smiled. "Good. Hopefully this will be the end of it then."

Risa stepped forward, wrapped her arms around Dane, and pressed an ear against his chest. The heartbeat was steady and strong. *Pulse rate of about 60,* she guessed. As they swayed side to side, Dane rubbed a hand through Risa's curls and rested his chin on top of her head. Releasing a contented breath, Risa drew back, stood on her toes, and puckered her lips. After a long kiss, she let her feet go flat and rested a palm on either side of Dane's stubbly face. "I'm going to miss you a lot."

"I'll miss you too." Dane's spring-sky eyes shone. "Don't wait too long to come up and see me, okay?"

"How 'bout tomorrow?"

He chuckled. "*I* won't even be in Nashville until tomorrow night, but we'll make it happen soon."

"Good."

Hand in hand, they walked to the front of the building and followed the sidewalk to Dane's car. After stepping onto the street, they shuffled to the driver's door, where he turned and said, "All right. For real this time."

Risa blocked the possibility that this would be their final goodbye, focusing on the moment. "Okay." She pinched his forearm. "Drive safe."

Dane smirked. "Don't tell me what to do." He kissed Risa's forehead and rubbed her cheek before opening the door and climbing inside. With folded arms, Risa stepped onto the sidewalk. Her chest grew heavy as the engine rattled to life, and Dane leaned over the passenger seat, blowing a kiss out the window.

Summoning a smile, Risa blew one back.

When the call came, Kody was sitting on a bench at an Arkansas truck stop, staring at the sprawling nothing and chewing a peanut butter cracker. Swallowing, he reached into his coat pocket and answered the phone. "Hello."

Dane's voice lacked its usual vitality. "What's up, Kody?"

"Almost to Tennessee. You?"

"Man, I've had a crazy morning."

Like his first time hearing a song he'd recorded, Kody listened with a pride catalyzed by the knowledge that he was the reason for Dane's listless delivery. His symphony of manipulation floated beautifully through the speaker.

"First, I walk out to my car and see that Risa's ex has slashed my tires." Kody's upper lip twitched. "So she and I got some junkyard ones and threw 'em on the car. And that's all good. But then—get *this*, man. I get back to my RV, and someone has just *destroyed* my windshield. I mean, like, absolutely obliterated it. No way I'd be able to see out of the thing."

"What?" Kody cued his acting skills. "Does that mean you won't be able to make the session?"

"Not necessarily."

Kody's surprise was now real. "How will you get to Nashville?"

"You should've seen it," Dane said proudly. "I leaned out the side window and drove the RV to a place that can fix the windshield, but they won't be able to get to it till tomorrow. But there's no way I'm gonna miss that session with you and Red. So I'm gonna drive up in the car, haul ass. I'm leaving Dripping Springs now."

Kody's thoughts whirled as Dane continued, "After we're done recording, I'll do a couple days of pedicabbing up there and drive back down to Texas to grab the RV. Actually, it's kinda cool how it all worked out, 'cuz I'll be able to hang with Risa again, and, who knows, maybe I'll even stay down in Austin for a while. Like you were saying, I could check out the pedicab scene there, see how things go." He paused. "Plus, I can't ignore these signs, man. It's like the Everything is trying to keep me in Texas."

Kody fought the urge to smash his phone on the sidewalk. "Why don't you just stay then?"

"I already told you. I've gotta record with you guys. Can't miss this opportunity."

"When will you be in Nashville?"

"Tomorrow afternoon." Dane paused. "Oh! Also, I was thinking, if you don't wanna sleep in the van, we could split a cheap motel room, save us both some money."

Like clouds parting, Kody's thoughts cleared. "Okay. Let's do that."

"Cool, man. I'll call you when I'm coming through Memphis. And, hopefully, I'll have some updates on the RV by then too. Turns out the guy who was camping near me got a look at whoever busted the windshield."

A tightening inside. "What?"

"Yeah. There was a note under my wiper saying to call him. I left a message but haven't heard back yet."

"Did he say what the person looked like?"

"No. He got a pretty good look at the guy though, so he'll give me a description and I can add that to the police report. Maybe they'll be able to figure out who it was and get me some cash, 'cuz that windshield repair won't be cheap."

Kody licked crumbs from his teeth. "Good news."

"Yeah. Honestly, I'd just like to be in a room alone with that dickhead for five minutes. It'd be worth paying for the repair just to lay him out."

Kody's brow grew hot. "Keep me posted."

"I will, man. See you in Music City."

They hung up, and Kody watched a station wagon full of useless people trundle away from the pump.

Ooooh, ain't it magic.

Kody stuffed a cracker into his mouth and chewed loudly to drown the melody. In the spaces between crunches, Dane's tune persisted, stabbing Kody's brain like a sonic sword. He clenched his jaw and stood. Then he walked into the station to buy some beer.

"Who would do something like that?" Risa asked.

Dane steered with one hand while holding the phone with the other. "I don't know. I only talked to two people at that campsite when I first parked there, a couple of rich hippies from Atlanta who seemed really cool. And I don't see how Vithu could have known about the RV unless he followed me all the way out there."

"God. I hope he didn't go *that* far," Risa replied. "If it wasn't him, though, why would it have happened on the same night as the tires?"

"Maybe it didn't. I was at your place for pretty much the whole time I was in Texas, so it could have happened whenever." Squinting to see through the drizzly night, Dane came upon a blinking construction sign that told him to merge right. He slowed down and took his place in a long line of brake lights. "Good news is I'll be back in Austin next week."

"Yay!" Risa stopped herself. "I mean, I'm glad you're coming down. Not that your windshield got smashed."

"Wait a second ..."

"Oh, shut up."

"It was *you*, wasn't it?"

Risa laughed. "You got me. I don't know why you waste your time with this music stuff. Clearly, your calling is detective work."

"I'm sending a car to arrest you."

"Can you wait till ten? I've got to apply lotion to this old woman's butt, and she's really counting on me."

"For her, I'll hold off."

"Sweet of you."

The car idled in the rain, and Dane accelerated the wipers. "All right, I'll let you get to moisturizing. Text you tomorrow when I settle in Nashville."

"Exciting!"

"Have fun rubbing those ancient cheeks."

Risa made a gagging noise and hung up.

Kody sulked in a camping chair beside the van. The relentless hiss of a late-night downpour was punctuated by blasts of thunder that echoed through the empty parking garage. With the guitar resting on his thigh, he stared across the space, through an opening in the side of the structure. Cypress leaves bounced as heavy raindrops struck like bullets shot from a hostile sky.

Kody reached down, grabbed a tall can of beer, and lifted it to his mouth. After a tongue-numbing gulp, he set the can on the ground and fished the phone from his pocket. Opening the banking app, he checked his balance and considered the number. Never in his life had he possessed so much money. Each dollar was a testament to a year's worth of gigs endured and countless hours slaved away in the warehouse. Not to mention the money he'd made with Dane, and the last bit he'd secured from the pawn shop on Lebanon Pike. And, in two days, nearly every penny would be gone.

Small price to pay, Kody concluded as he set the phone on the concrete.

This recording session would be his life's most meaningful opportunity, his time to shine. He'd played the scenario out a million times. He would work with Red, who would introduce him to the right people, and these higher-ups would recognize his talents and put him on tour.

That would be the start of everything.

Kody Logan would be somebody.

Closing his eyes, he pictured himself stepping onto the tour bus after some stadium-size gig, pouring a strong drink as he recalled the glorious roar of the crowd, basking in the realization that all that noise had been made for him ...

Suddenly, Kody was seated at a bar, some dingy place he'd played a hundred times. The sparsely attended performance had just ended, and he was scrawling mistakes into his notebook when two giggling girls sat beside him.

One said to the other, "Did you hear that Dane Sorensen is headlining the festival next weekend?"

The second girl grabbed the first one's arm. "We *need* to go!"

Kody's eyes snapped open, and he pulled a cigarette from his pocket. He lit it and took a drag.

Red hadn't been open to the idea of dropping Dane from the session.

And Dane hadn't wanted to stay in Austin for Risa.

The slashed tires hadn't stopped Dane.

Neither had the broken windshield.

Exhaling smoke, Kody pondered his options.

I could ignore Dane, stop answering his calls and messages.

    He would contact Red.

I could disable Dane's car.

    He would find a ride to the studio.

I could tell him the session has been canceled or delayed.

    Again, Dane would reach out to Red.

Staring through the opening in the side of the garage, Kody watched God's piss pour from the sky. His breathing hastened, and the intensifying pressure felt like a python tightening around his lungs.

Kody sucked on the cigarette.

The fire calmed him.

A dog barked in the night, and a ghostly cloud seeped from Kody's lips as he closed his eyes. In the darkness, he saw the RV, saw the pit bull. He relived the chase, felt the brain-quaking panic. He remembered ducking into the bushes, tripping. Flipping over as the dog charged ferociously, obeying its primal urges.

It was survival, Kody told himself. *Him or me.*

Opening his eyes, he thought about how easy it had been to do what was necessary. He remembered feeling nothing as he had wiped the blade clean.

Him or me.

A monstrous clap of thunder rocked the sticky air, and Kody lifted the beer to his lips. When the can was empty, he crushed it and tossed it onto the concrete.

59

Risa jolted awake, her skin tight with terror. The room was dark, and she heard footsteps in the apartment above. As she turned beneath the comforter, the nightmare surged back.

Risa felt the sandy beach beneath her as she lay on the towel. She opened her eyes, and the sun was like a spotlight in the blue sky. Beside the sun was a large black blob.

The dread crept in.

To distract herself, she sat up and scanned the scene. Children squealed with delight as they splashed in the surf. On the hot sand, four dudes threw a Frisbee between them, and a young couple walked hand-in-hand along the water's edge. Beyond them, a wetsuit-wearing surfer ducked beneath a breaking wave and kicked his way toward the horizon. Down the beach was a long pier. At the end of it, several people sat with fishing lines cast into the water.

Halfway down the pier, someone waved exuberantly toward the beach. Risa cupped a hand over her eyes and recognized the person as Dane. She smiled and waved back as Dane curled his biceps and lifted a board-short-wearing leg to rest his bare foot on a horizontal plank of the railing. As Risa snickered, a huge, shadowy figure stalked up behind Dane, who was now squatting down and up, down and up, looking at Risa and flexing. With one violent motion, the shadow clasped a massive hand around Dane's neck, and Risa sprinted across the sand, screaming for someone to help.

People on towels stared at her. Children went silent. The Frisbee fell to the ground.

Risa darted toward the pier, kicking sand while Dane struggled to breathe and fought to break free from the shadow's grip. Risa ran up the wooden ramp, across the boards. Before she could intervene, the shadow reached down and scooped Dane's legs, picking him up like a flailing child and heaving him over the railing.

"No!" Risa screamed, panicked. She leaned over, searching the water.

When Dane didn't surface, Risa looked around frantically and saw that the shadow had vanished. A gull squawked as it soared overhead. Nearby, an old Vietnamese fisherman was seated on an overturned plastic bucket, smoking a cigarette, staring at Risa.

"Don't just sit there!" she pleaded. "Do something!"

Expressionless, the fisherman plucked the cigarette from his mouth and flicked it into the crest of a rolling wave.

The sound of Dane's violin echoed inside the cement tunnel that ran beneath the road. Upon arriving in Nashville, his first mission had been to find a place where he could eat some of the city's famous hot chicken. After satisfying his craving, he'd found a grassy park where he could run through the songs he'd be playing the following day. Not wanting to disturb the kids playing baseball, he had concluded the tunnel at the far end of the field would make a perfect practice space.

Beads of sweat clung to his forehead as the muggy air filled his lungs. Rocking back and forth, he tugged the bow across the strings, sending divine reverberations along his spine that rippled outward at the speed of sound, electrifying every nerve. With eyes shut, he became music, radiating beyond the fleshly confines of his body, bouncing off the rounded walls of the tunnel and co-mingling with the photonic frenzy of the sunny afternoon. Suddenly, Dane's ringtone snapped him from his trance, and he set the violin and bow on the concrete beside a trail of green sludge. He reached into his pocket to check the phone.

"*Bonita*," he answered.

"Hi, *guapo*."

"How's the day?"

"A patient tried to punch me in the face and then spit on me after we restrained him."

Dane chuckled. "Never a dull moment."

"That's definitely *not* true, but there are a lot of interesting ones." Risa sighed. "You make it to Nashville?"

"I did. Ate some food and now practicing for the session tomorrow."

"Are you giddy?"

Dane nodded. "It's pretty unreal. Can't believe I'm actually gonna be playing in that studio."

"I can't wait to hear all about it."

"I'll take some videos while I'm there and send 'em to you."

"Groovy. It'll be fun to see where the magic happens." Risa took a bite of something. "Did you meet up with Kody?"

"No. I'll see him at the motel."

"Oh, right. You guys are having a sleepover."

Dane rubbed his eye, itchy from the pollen. "Yup. Gonna check in around five."

"Single bed?" Risa teased.

"You know it. I'll be the big spoon."

"Send me a video of that too."

"Will do."

In the distance, the crack of a metallic baseball bat rang out, followed by the sound of children cheering.

"Well," Risa said. "I don't want to keep you from practice, but I just wanted to say, 'good luck,' and I know you'll do great."

"I'm kissing your forehead through the phone."

"Mmmm." She lowered her voice. "I wish you'd do more."

A smile crept across Dane's face. "Well, then—"

"I've gotta go before I get too excited."

He laughed. "Sounds good."

"Have so much fun tomorrow."

"I will."

Dane hung up and looked out through the tunnel's opening. On the baseball field, a young boy chased a line drive toward the fence. After watching the kid scoop the ball, Dane opened the streaming app on his phone and queued up a Cal Walker song. Then he set the phone on the concrete, picked up his instrument, and began to play along.

With the guitar bag hanging from his shoulder, Kody dodged raindrops in the dark as he carried his backpack and a bottle of water across the parking lot and up the stairs of the slummy motel. While he passed the rooms on the second floor, a group of umbrella-wielding women in the parking lot chattered loudly about a music venue where they were headed. Outside of room 207, Kody clenched the water bottle between his legs and knocked.

Dane's voice called from inside, "Yo!"

Kody reached into his coat pocket and lifted his hand—coat covering his palm—to twist the knob. The door swung inward, revealing Dane, who was stretched out on a twin bed wearing only boxer shorts. His hands rested behind his head.

Lowering his gaze, Kody mumbled, "Hey," and closed the door with his foot.

A witty one-liner erupted from the TV, followed by a choir of canned laughter.

"Feels like Christmas Eve," Dane declared with a broad smile.

Kody set his backpack on the unoccupied bed and dropped the guitar bag from his shoulder before resting it against the wall. He sulked across the room and plopped onto the recliner beside the TV. "It's close." He opened the water bottle and took a gulp.

"Do you ever take that coat off?" Dane teased.

Kody set the bottle on the carpet and leaned back in the chair, staring at the ceiling and wondering what had caused the pervasive brown stain on the once-pristine white tiles.

After a long, responseless silence, Dane sat up. "What's going on, man?" He stuffed a pillow between himself and the wall. "You nervous about tomorrow?"

Kody maintained his upward gaze. "I just hope I don't die before this is finished."

Dane fought the urge to chuckle. "The recording?"

Kody glared at him. "Before the songs are released."

"What makes you say that? You got cancer or something?"

Kody furrowed his brows. "My whole life has led up to this session. I've worked very hard to make all of this happen."

"So ..." Dane tapped a finger on the mattress. "Are you stoked then? How do you feel? Now that you're only—" He glanced at the digital clock and looked back at Kody. "Eleven hours away."

"I don't."

Dane scratched his stubbly jaw. "Huh?"

"I don't *feel* anything."

Dane nodded contemplatively. "Okay, well ... Maybe you're just getting yourself in the zone. You know, like an athlete ready to step onto the field."

Kody slid a hand into his coat pocket. "Maybe."

More laughter from the TV.

"Hey, let me ask you something." Dane scooted to the edge of the bed and hung his legs over. "Why do *you* play music?"

Staring at the grimy carpet, Kody thought about how Father used to spit phlegm onto his own bedroom floor. "I don't really know anymore." He wished Dane would evaporate, perhaps transform into a pillow or some piece of furniture incapable of asking questions. "Sometimes I wonder if it's just a way to hide from the world but still participate in it." Kody ran his finger along the object in his pocket. "When I'm on stage, I—I can close my eyes and disappear, become a song." He looked at Dane. "And in that state, I, well… that's how I feel okay relating to people, how I connect with them. Without having to talk, without all the fakeness and fear."

A commotion broke out on the TV show, tinny voices clamoring for attention.

"Music is pure." Kody peeked over his shoulder to watch the soft, soulless actors. "It's real." His leg began to bounce. "More so than most conversations I have. More than most people I meet." He refocused on Dane. "Music is everything to me."

An impish grin spread across Dane's face. "I don't know, man. There's some garbage music out there too."

Kody's leg stopped bouncing.

"Sorry." Dane rubbed the back of his head. "Didn't mean to trample your moment there."

Kody exhaled laboriously. "I envy people like you."

Dane raised his eyebrows.

"People who can just go through life and enjoy it for what it is." Kody picked at the arm of the chair. "I can't do that. I never feel good enough, never feel like I've done enough." His voice was flat. "I don't ever feel like I've earned it."

Dane crossed his legs on the mattress. "Earned what? Feeling good?"

Kody nodded.

Dane rubbed his palms together as if he were conjuring the right response. "Well, Kody—" The phone rang. "Oh." He glanced over his shoulder. "Gimme one sec." He stood and walked to the nightstand where, upon seeing the screen, he snatched the bunched-up T-shirt from the bed and hastily slid it on. "I've gotta get this." He poked his head through the neck hole. "It's the guy who saw my windshield get smashed."

After wiggling into his shorts, Dane grabbed the phone and headed for the door.

62

There has to be another way.
I'm just not thinking hard enough.

Think, idiot.

A salesman's elastic voice rang out from the TV.
"Cleans any stain in seconds. Just spray, wait, and ... voila! Mess-be-gone!"

But if—in the long run—my life doesn't mean anything,
if none of our lives actually mean anything,
then it doesn't matter what I do.
There is no God to judge.
There is only us and what we think about our actions.

We, together, are God.

"Coffee spilt on the cushions? Easy as one, two, three!"

Our collective mind is the hard drive.
Which means that when all the humans are gone,
all information, as we know it, ceases to exist.

Therefore, if I'm the only one who knows something,
then the reality of that "something" can be whatever I make it.
Whatever I want it to be.
Whatever I need it to be.

"Red wine on the carpet? No problem!"

63

When Dane reentered the room, Kody was seated on the recliner, writing in his pocket notebook. Dane closed the door, marched toward the bed, and grabbed the remote, which he pointed at the TV. The screen went blank, and he sat on the end of the bed, facing Kody, who avoided eye contact while stuffing the notebook into his coat.

"Was it you?" Dane tossed the remote onto the bed beside him.

Kody slid the pen into a pocket of his jeans and glanced apprehensively at Dane.

"Tell you what," Dane said. "I'm pretty sure there aren't many people in Dripping Springs, Texas, with"—he extended a finger for each characteristic—"brown hair. A big black coat in the middle of May." He pressed a thumb into his neck. "A *snake* tattoo on their fucking neck." Dane stood and paced the floor, running a hand through his hair, turning toward Kody. "What's up, man?" He held his palms up and moved closer. "Not gonna say anything?"

Kody glowered, hot blood pumping.

"Was it you or not?" Dane demanded.

"Yes."

Clenching his jaw, Dane took an extended breath and stepped forward. "Why would you do that?"

Kody maneuvered a hand into his coat pocket. "Because I don't want you here."

Dane's features twisted. "What?"

"Exactly what I said." Kody sneered and leaned forward. "I. Don't. Want you here."

"Here, like, Nashville?"

Kody nodded.

Dane moved closer. "So you smashed my windshield?"

Amused that Dane still didn't hadn't figured out about the tires, Kody drew back. "Yes."

"Why didn't you just tell me not to come?"

"Red wants you to play."

"You introduced me to him!"

"I changed my mind."

"You changed your *mind*?" Dane sprung forward, one hand grabbing each arm of the recliner. "So just change your mind then. And tell me about it." A vein bulged in his neck. "But instead, you decide to take some chicken-shit, passive-aggressive way out. You try to make me the one to—" Dane pushed himself back from the chair and waved a hand dismissively. "You know what?" He walked over to his backpack, picked it up, and pulled the straps over his shoulders. He knelt to grab his violin case from beneath the bed.

"What are you doing?" Kody asked.

Dane sat on the mattress and slid his socks on, then shoes. "Leaving."

"That's it?"

Tying his laces, Dane stared at Kody in disbelief. "Normally, I'd knock your ass out." He finished lacing and stood, exhaling heartily. "Matter of fact, I'm having a real tough time not doing that." He bit his lip and glanced toward the wall, then refocused on Kody. "But you're pathetic." Dane's words poked the Thing. "You're a waste of talent, man, a waste of life." It awakened with a hateful hiss. "You said it yourself. You can't enjoy shit, 'cuz all you're doing is chasing some light at the end of a tunnel that you may never even see." Dane shook his head. "And there's probably nothing I could do to you that would make you feel worse than you already do." He took a step forward. "Matter of fact, if I *did* hit you, then you'd probably find a way to twist the story in your fucked-up head and make me the bad guy."

Dane grabbed his violin case from the bed. "I'm not gonna give you that." He pointed the instrument at Kody. "I know there's a conscience in you, Kody. I've seen it. And I hope someday, when there's no music to block the sound of it, I hope that thing swallows you up." He poked a finger into his neck. "Like that stupid tattoo of yours: the snake eating its own tail." He released a single-syllable chuckle. "You probably see that as some metaphor for humanity, right?"

Kody stared coldly, possessed by the ferocious flailing inside. It bashed against his liver, then lungs, trying desperately to burst its way out.

"Seems like a self-fulfilling prophecy to me." Dane shrugged. "Maybe some part of you knew, deep down, the failure of a man you'd become. Then it told you to brand a symbol on your skin for the world to see." He smirked. "But you'd be the only one too blind to recognize what it really meant." A contemplative pause, then a nod in Kody's direction. "It's *you* that you hate—you who's ruining your only life—not the people you hide from, or our species as a whole." A look of concern overtook Dane, possibly remorse, like he'd been too stern with a rescued dog who'd ruined the rug. "Besides all that, though, I think ..." He hesitated. "Well, honestly, man, I just hope you find whatever you're looking for."

As Dane walked toward the door, the Thing forced its way into Kody's throat and slammed its head repeatedly against the back of his grinding teeth. Breathing deeply, deliberately, he swallowed saliva to wash it back down and commanded it to coil in silence. Reclining in the chair, he looked at the ceiling. The brown stain seemed to be spreading. Kody's heart thumped in his fingers as he folded his hands together, stroking the Thing with the soothing knowledge that their plan had worked.

Smoothly, easily.

Circling his thumbs around one another, Kody contemplated how he would find a replacement fiddler.

Email Red.

Visualizing what he would say, Kody remembered that Dane had Red's contact info, and his pulse quickened as he pictured the producer receiving a phone call from Dane.

"Hey, Red, I've gotta tell you something ..."

Imagining the producer's irate reaction, Kody's mind raced.

What if he won't work with me?

What if no one will?

Venomous fangs flared within. *What if I'm blacklisted?*

As Dane grabbed the door handle, Kody pulled the knife from his coat.

This is one of those defining moments, where a single decision changes the course of everything.

He stood, taking brisk steps across the carpet.

Him or me.

The blade penetrated Dane's shoulder with ease, gliding in beside the bone. As Kody withdrew the knife, adrenaline shot through him like an electrical current, erecting hairs and invigorating every muscle. With a pained yell, Dane wheeled around and swung the violin case. Dodging the attack, Kody saw confusion in Dane's eyes. *The element of surprise.* He lunged forward, slashing at Dane's chest but missing.

Stumbling backward, Dane hit the bedside table and knocked the lamp to the floor. Kody threw the knife to the ground and picked up the lamp, raising it above his head with both hands. As Dane lifted his arms to defend himself, Kody roared and brought the lamp crashing down on Dane's head. Unconscious, he slumped forward and landed sideways on the floor. Blood trickled down his face. Tossing the lamp aside, Kody bent to grab the knife.

Someone must've heard all that noise.

Hurriedly, Kody flipped Dane over and stabbed at his chest, but the blade wouldn't penetrate beyond the ribs. Panicking, Kody raised the knife and plunged it into Dane's stomach. As he pulled it out, specks of blood spattered the curtains and wallpaper.

No time. Go.

Heart pounding louder than the ringing in his ears, Kody raced across the carpet and picked up his backpack. He pulled the straps over his shoulders and grabbed his guitar bag. As he turned to leave, he remembered the water bottle and wheeled around to collect it. After stashing it in his coat pocket, Kody crossed the carpet and opened the door with the coat covering his hand.

Tires hissed on the road below, speeding across the soaked asphalt.

Kody stepped into the drizzling night and shut the door, sprinting down the splashing stairs. As he crossed the parking lot, he glanced around, clutching the knife against his stomach. His hands trembled. His breaths were shallow. He might vomit.

After opening the van's back hatch, Kody stuffed the guitar bag beside the bed frame. He set the knife on the bumper and opened a garbage bag of dirty clothes. Rifling through, he found a white shirt, wrapped the knife, and jammed it into a plastic tub beside a blanket-wrapped speaker. Closing the hatch, he heard a chest-rattling cough from across the parking lot and turned to see a shadowy someone standing on the second floor. With one hand, they lifted an electronic smoking device to their lips. A red dot glowed in the blackness like the target-finding light of a sniper's rifle. The other hand held a phone horizontally, pointed in Kody's direction.

VI
Floating Toward the Drain

64

"Not that one!"** Father's voice sagged, heavy with vodka, as young Dane peeked over his shoulder for the clarification that struck like a verbal slap. "What part of 'the big white rock' don't you understand?"

Barefoot in the neighbor's beauty bark, Dane glanced toward their living-room window, hoping somebody would come outside and put an end to this early-evening mission. His gaze drifted toward the open-top trailer in their driveway, loaded with sticks and leaves where the angry bees lived.

"Today!" Father's alcoholic bark sounded like that of the dog with the long paw-nails at the end of the cul-de-sac. Ducking beneath the rhododendron, Kody reached out and rolled the basketball-sized stone toward him, stepping out of its way before it could crush his toes.

Bending his knees to hoist it. Legs trembling as he hefted it toward Father at the top of the porch stairs. Father, who gulped from the bottle, wearing a long black coat and thick sunglasses on an overcast evening. Streetlights would come on soon. An hour after that, Mom would come home.

Step up. Then another.

Step up. One more.

"My little Nordic strongman. World's strongest strongman!" Father stood aside so young Dane could struggle past, red-faced and determined. "Throw it on the couch."

The cat brushed affectionately against Kody's leg as he crossed the carpet, wrists weakening, shoulders burning with stubborn blood. He let out a groan as he heaved forward, and the rock plopped onto a cushion that sank like Andy's trampoline.

Double-bounce. Smelly feet. Wash them in the downstairs sink.

Bloody Band-aid in the soap holder.

Door locked now. Banging for escape. Mom is screaming on the other side, and Father is too. He's louder. Mom is bawling.

"I want a hug!" Kody cries, pounding on the hollow wooden door.

I could kick through it.

Crashing glass and a metallic thud.

"Don't you EVER say that!"

Door is steel now, thick and sturdy like that of a bank vault. Window too small. Metal walls and bright buzzing bulbs on the squinting ceiling.

"I want a hug!" Young Dane is sobbing.

Flashing red-and-blue lights on the midnight street outside. Peeking through venetian blinds. *Cars like my toys.*

Door opens. Blue man with a gun. Hallway is a shadowy tunnel. Mom is a long maroon skirt with cold toes on the kitchen floor. Blue men around her. She raises her mascara-streaked face and sees Kody. Her eyes sour with sorrow as she reaches an arm toward him. "Come here, baby."

Icy concrete beneath my feet. "Can't they turn up the heat in this place?" No light switch. *They'll shut them off at ten.*

Mom draws Dane tightly against her warm body, clutching him like a sniffling teddy bear. She makes a long noise that sounds like "he he he," but she's not laughing.

Blue man's radio goes *Tssssh.*

Kody rubs a hand through Mom's wet hair. She looks at him. "Whatever happens." Her eyes are glistening. "Just know that I love you." On the kitchen floor beside her, the spilled chocolate-milk powder makes a brown blemish on the once-pristine white tile.

65

Forehead slick with sweat, Kody shot upright with a gasp. He ripped the sleep mask from his eyes, and the confines of his misty-windowed cage closed in on him like the jaws of some giant beast. The previous night's events rushed into his mind.

The motel. The knife.

Him.

Gulping for air, he wondered if he'd completed the task, wondered if he'd left evidence. While opening the curtain and sliding the door, Kody castigated himself for not checking Dane's pulse, for not making sure the deed was done. He replayed the struggle in his mind and recalled grabbing the lamp with bare hands—with bare fingertips. His stomach turned in on itself like a shame-sucking black hole.

I can't even do that *right.*

In the hazy morning air, Kody sat on the running board and scanned the suburban neighborhood. The van was parked in the driveway of a house undergoing a remodel, and a large construction dumpster occupied the middle of a yard that had been stripped to dirt. No crew was on site.

A woman in athletic clothes regarded Kody as she bounded up the sidewalk. Tying his shoe, Kody waved, and the woman averted her eyes, quickening her pace.

She knows.

Wearing his flannel pajama pants and a sweatshirt, Kody stood and lit a cigarette. He inspected the two-story brick house covered in ivy and noticed that the side door was cracked open. *Dane's head was cracked open.* Sucking the smoke, he coughed before dropping the cigarette to the dirt. After circling around the van, he popped the tailgate and grabbed his backpack and a towel. He closed the hatch and walked toward the house, glancing over his shoulder, checking for neighbors. He walked up the concrete steps and peeked inside. The living room was empty.

"Hello!"

No answer.

Kody looked over his shoulder. No activity on the street.

The cookie-cutter houses were silent.

He slipped inside, shutting the door behind him. The place was frigid and smelled of mildew. Wishing he'd brought the knife, Kody stood still and listened for human noises. Hearing none, he crept toward the hallway. The bathroom was the first door on the right. A bare curtain rod hung above a rust-stained tub. On the floor, black and white tiles were marked with splotches of grime. On the toilet lid was a stack of napkins.

Kody hung the towel on the shower rod and laid his backpack on the ground. Resting a hand on the rim of the tub, he leaned to twist the handle. The faucet coughed before spewing dirty water onto the yellowing porcelain. After a moment, the flow became clear and steady. Kody reached out to feel the water. *Cold.* He turned the other handle, waited a moment, and felt the water again. *Still cold.*

Picturing a crew of workers bursting through the door at any moment, Kody removed his clothes. He unzipped his backpack and set the soap and shampoo on the rim of the tub before reaching over to pull the tab on the faucet. The pipes gurgled. The shower head dripped. There was a loud hiss, and several streams spat forth, stirring the dirt at the back of the tub, which floated swiftly toward the drain.

Kody stepped into the shower. The icy water felt like needles pricking his skin. As he turned to wet his face, hair, and chest, the water dripped between his legs and shrunk his genitals to the size they'd been when he was six. After wetting the soap, he lathered it on the necessary areas before shampooing. Working fingers through his hair, he saw Dane's face streaked with red. Positioning his head beneath the freezing streams, the water washed his mind clean. *Kody the Killer.* Imaginary blood trickled down his legs and began to swirl around the circular grate.

He stopped the shower.

Stepping over the side of the tub, he toweled himself off and reached into his backpack for jeans, underwear, and a T-shirt. After putting these on, along with some fresh socks and his shoes, he stuffed the bar of soap into a dirty sock and stashed it, along with the shampoo, in the backpack. *Fled the motel in a hurry. Did I forget something?* He slid the backpack over his shoulders, grabbed the dirty clothes, and went outside.

Emerging from the house, he saw two pre-teen girls climbing into the back of a sedan across the street while their father stood beside the open driver's door. The back doors shut in succession, and the man considered Kody with suspicious eyes.

Descending the stairs quickly, Kody opened the van door and threw his pack onto the passenger seat before leaning inside where he couldn't be seen. Once the neighbors had driven away, Kody went to the van's rear, opened the hatch, and put his dirty clothes into the garbage bag. *Murder weapon.* After closing the tailgate, he went to the driver's side and climbed in. He shut the door, started the engine, and put it in reverse. Suddenly, an idea struck, and he parked and got out. He circled around, raised the hatch, and reached into a plastic tub, where he found the rolled-up white shirt stained with dried blood. Taking it out, he strode across the dirt, searching the neighborhood for witnesses. Seeing none, he tossed the T-shirt-wrapped knife into the construction dumpster.

It landed with a metallic thud.

66

"Good to finally meet you," Red Smith greeted with an easy smile. He extended a hand, which Kody shook nervously before the producer stepped aside. "Come on in."

With the guitar slung on his back, Kody walked into a tall, hardwood-floored room and closed the door behind him. Beneath a worn blue baseball cap, Red's eyes gleamed like those of a longtime friend. His fitted white T-shirt highlighted an impressive physique for a man of almost seventy. Other than some stubborn remnants of brown in his mustache, Red's hair and beard were a silvery gray. He gestured toward a slender, blond woman who was setting up drums in the corner. "This is Darcy."

Images of Darcy on stage with Cal Walker—their band playing for a sea of screaming fans—flashed through Kody's mind as she wiggled a rack tom onto its stand and said, "Hiya," with a quick bob of the chin.

Starstruck, Kody waved and said, "Hello." The greeting came out scratchy. He cleared his dry throat and tried again, stronger this time. "Hello."

Before Kody's overwhelming inadequacy could take hold, Red said, "Here," and opened a sliding glass door on the far side of the room. As Kody crossed the hardwood, he inspected a collection of vintage amplifiers and lined up against the wall.

I wonder if Cal used any of these.

He stepped over the sliding-door track into a cozy vocal booth padded with soundproof foam. Through another door was the studio's control room. Against the back wall of this modest space were two wooden cabinets loaded with plug-ins and effects. Across from the cabinets stood the room's centerpiece—a magnificent recording console, which, with its myriad dials, buttons, and sliders, resembled the controls of some spaceship destined for distant worlds. On either side of the console were two large speakers perched atop tall stands. Between these was a window that looked into the drum room.

Red sat in an office chair in front of the console and gestured toward a small couch in the corner. "Take a seat."

Kody slid the guitar bag from his shoulder and leaned it against a wall decorated with gold and platinum records, many of which he recognized.

Reaching beneath the console, Red grabbed two water bottles and turned around. "Here ya go." He tossed one across the room, and Kody tried to catch it, but he fumbled, and the bottle fell to the floor. He recalled a Little League groundball taking an unexpected bounce into his nose, cracking cartilage as the opposing team jeered and laughed. With a shake of his head, he reached to retrieve the bottle.

"Which song did you want to start with?" Red took a drink.

Twisting the cap, Kody said, "'Sixteen Voices'?"

Red nodded. "I like that one."

Kody sipped his water as the pride swelled.

"You mind running it for me?" Red set his bottle on the floor and grabbed a notepad and pen.

"Okay." Kody placed his water on a cabinet, sat on the couch, and began to unzip his guitar bag.

"Dane was coming with you this morning, correct?"

Kody's throat tightened, and he swallowed sand, pulling the guitar from the bag. "He was supposed to."

Red dug the phone from his pocket and checked his messages. "And you haven't heard from him?"

Laying the guitar across his thigh, Kody shook his head and saw motel drapes spattered with blood. "No."

"Odd." Red looked curiously at Kody. "Well, it'll take Darcy and me a little while to get these drums going." He glanced at his phone again. "Let's give him an hour to show up or reach out." Red returned the phone to his pocket. "Otherwise, we can probably get someone else to come last minute." He waved the pen. "If not, we can always track fiddle later."

With a simmering satisfaction, Kody forced the gore from his mind. "Okay." He closed his eyes and started to strum. In the blackness, reality sank in, and his heart thudded against his ribs.

I'm in Nashville. With Red Smith.

During the first verse, Kody's voice trembled as he thought back to the drudgery of his old life, when he had longed for escape, begged for something new. Thinking back on the last few years, he saw that his decision to play music by the food trucks had become a life of travel and performing—a destiny of his own creation.

I did it, Kody realized while switching chords. *I made a living playing music.*

The memory of Father's voice grumbled in his head, telling him he wouldn't be able to do it, telling him it wasn't practical. Lyrics flowed unconsciously from Kody's lips as he imagined his dad sitting on the other side of the room, watching him now. Between slugs from the bottle, Father surveyed the studio, inspecting the awards and expensive equipment, watching curiously as Red scrawled notes onto his pad and tapped a foot on the hardwood. Then Father heard the knock on the studio door.

Red stood up. "That might be Dane."

Kody stopped strumming and opened his eyes.

"Sorry, Kody." Red strode across the control room.

Kody's insides churned. *It can't be Dane.* He heard the studio door open, and two male voices exchanged indistinguishable words with Red.

The bassist? Kody thought. *Keyboard player?*

When the producer came into the control room with two police officers, the kindness in Red's eyes had been hijacked by concern. Without saying a word, he sat in his chair and fixed his gaze on Kody.

Glancing up at the officers, Kody clenched his jaw.

"Sir, does the van out front belong to you?"

Feeling weightless, Kody nodded.

The officer placed a hand on his cuffs. "I'm going to ask you to stand slowly."

67

Risa's curls bounced as she marched across the polished linoleum.
I hope they know what they're doing here.

Entering a dimly lit room, she was struck by the sight of Dane propped up in the hospital bed with eyes closed, breathing shallowly. His head was wrapped with a thick bandage. Rebellious blond hairs protruded from the folds.

"Oh no." Risa's eyes moistened as she crossed the floor. Standing over Dane, she inspected the medical equipment—the IV bag and tube running down to his arm, where it was connected to one of her favorite veins. She wished she could've been the one to insert the needle.

Dane's eyes opened slowly, and his lips curled upward. "*Bonita.*"

"Mmmm." Risa stooped to kiss him on the cheek. Pulling away, she rubbed a palm gently across his hospital-gown-covered chest.

"You were right." Dane winced in pain.

Withdrawing her hand, Risa cocked her head to the side.

"About Kody. About the darkness."

"Shhh." Risa put a finger to Dane's lips and inspected the bandage on his shoulder. "Jesus Christ," she whispered.

"Mm-hmm. They've got me on some *good* drugs though."

Risa grinned and shook her head.

"The juice is really good too." Dane reached up to press the call button. "Here. Let me get you some."

She clutched his arm and giggled. "No!"

"It's so tasty though."

"I believe you."

"How 'bout I just get some and you can have a sip?"

Risa leaned closer. "How about I go get it, so the nurse doesn't have to come all the way just for that."

Dane waved his hand. "Never mind. Stay here instead."

He was behaving like Melanie's toddler. "You *are* high, aren't you?"

"Yes, ma'am." Dane nodded. "And you came all the way up here to see me."

"I did."

Dane lifted the bottom of his gown and scratched his pale thigh. "Why didn't you just wait till I came back down to Austin?"

"Well." Risa knelt beside the bed. "It wouldn't be fair if you came to Texas twice in a row, would it?" She traced a fingernail along his forearm.

A sluggish grin spread across Dane's face. "When do you go back?"

"Don't worry about it."

Dane scooted over, grimacing. "Okay." He patted the empty space beside him, and Risa walked around to the other side of the bed, where, crawling in, she leaned her head against Dane's good shoulder and intertwined her fingers with his.

Dane's pulse pounded against her palm. "At least your heart rate is still good."

He began to laugh but stopped himself. "Aaah." He placed his free hand over his stomach and shook his head. "No being funny right now."

Risa tittered. "Deal."

Squeezing Dane's hand, she visualized the terrible scenario that had put him here, and, after a short deliberation, decided not to ask about it. *If he wants to talk about it, he will.*

The heart monitor chirped.

Beep, beep.

"Hey," Risa said as she sat up and looked at him. "I want to tell you something."

Dane's lazy eyes focused on her.

"The other day, after we had that psycho patient who spit on me, I started feeling really fed up with the hospital. I actually thought about walking out, but I decided I was just overreacting—which I was—but still, I started to feel trapped, like I was going to be dealing with people like that for the rest of my life."

"But you then *could* get a studly patient like me."

Risa smirked. "You're a nurse's dream." She let go of Dane's hand and rubbed his leg through the gown. "After my shift that day, I thought 'What do I have to lose?' So I went to the studio and grabbed a few of my paintings"—Dane grew a soft smile—"and I borrowed a little folding table from the photographer and a tablecloth. Then I went to the farmer's market on the east side to set up and see what happened."

Dane's eyebrows inched upward. "Yeah?"

Risa nodded.

"And?"

"Aaand." Risa rubbed her neck. "I only sold one little one."

Dane's eyes widened. "You sold one?" His smile grew broad and bright.

"Yeah, but I was there for a whole three hours, and only a handful of people stopped by—"

"Risa." Dane squeezed her fingers. "You sold a painting." He withdrew his hand. "That's awesome. Like, someone has a piece of you hanging up in their bedroom or dining room. They could even be looking at it right now. Or maybe they have some friends over, and they're standing in front of it with glasses of wine, saying"—he did his best pretentious-art-snob voice—"'Yes, it bears an uncanny resemblance to the early work of O'Keeffe.'"

Risa laughed. "Oh. So you can be funny right now, but I can't?"

Dane nodded, looking handsome even in his battered state. "Did you hand out some business cards?"

Risa thought back to the college-aged girl who had asked about a portrait for her mother's birthday. "A couple." She focused on Dane's tranquil eyes. "I want to thank you, though." She grabbed his hand. "For believing in me."

Dane radiated a grounded warmth. "Why didn't you tell me about this when it happened?"

Risa sighed. "I was embarrassed. I wanted to be able to say I went down there and sold all of my canvases and made a million dollars."

"Well, you sold one." He caressed her palm. "And that's a solid start."

Risa kissed Dane's cheek before returning her head to his shoulder. Inhaling wholly, she allowed the goodness to course through her like morphine and felt Dane's pulse in sync with the steady rhythm of the heart monitor.

Beep, beep, beep.

68

One of the inmates slammed his hands on the table, causing a twenty-dollar stack of poker chips to topple. "That's right!" He reached forward and scooped his winnings toward an already impressive haul. Seated around the table, three other prisoners hurled playful insults and tossed their cards to the center of the game. One of them collected the cards and began to shuffle the deck.

Seated at an adjacent table, Kody scribbled on a piece of jail-issued paper, wishing the men would shut up. Each time they yelled at one another or burst out in collective laughter, Kody's focus was shattered, and the Thing stirred with a hiss. Glaring at the men, he caught the attention of one, who snapped, "What?" and stared menacingly. The other two players turned to look at Kody, and the dealer began to dish out cards.

From the ceiling-mounted TV, a female news anchor reported an accident on I-65.

"Expect the congestion to last for the next several hours ..."

Kody dropped his gaze and concentrated on the pen.

"A poem for me?" the inmate asked.

Kody was silent.

"Hey," the inmate growled. "I'm talking to you."

"In other news," the anchor continued, "an arrest has been made in the assault of a twenty-eight-year-old man at a motel on Donelson Pike." Kody looked at the TV, where his mugshot filled the screen. "Thirty-year-old Kody Logan from Portland, Oregon, is being held in custody at Hill Detention Center in Nashville after his arrest at a local recording studio yesterday morning."

The inmates watched the screen, where Red Smith was being interviewed. "Well," he said into the microphone, "I'd been talking to him for the better part of a year now about coming to track. So he came in to do some songs, and not fifteen minutes into sitting down with me, the cops show up and take him away." Red shook his head. "Damn shame. Good writer."

A corner of Kody's mouth crept upward.

"That's not a poem he's making," the inmate said to the others. "It's a song." He stood and strutted toward Kody's table. When Kody pulled the paper toward himself, the inmate snatched the sheet. "Gimme that." Kody sized-up the other men, who watched him fixedly as the inmate folded the paper and grinned wickedly at Kody. "Thanks, baby." He kissed the air. "I'll read it tonight."

Other prisoners murmured and whispered as the inmate went back to his table. After he sat down, the dealer said, "Buck," and tossed a chip into the center of the game. As the other players followed suit, one of them nodded toward the inmate. "Read us your love letter."

The group's mirth triggered an intensifying pressure behind Kody's eyes. *Can a brain explode?* And he attempted to control the Feeling—tried to stifle it— but, like the rushing waters of a bursting dam, it gushed through him. Rivers of acid seared the inner walls of arteries and veins, cooking every cell to smoldering mush. There was no numbing substance with which he could extinguish the sensation, and no creative means through which it could be released. Tightening his grip on the pen, Kody watched the muscles in his hand tense around a pedicab handbrake. Then he focused on the TV.

"High chance of showers tomorrow morning," the pearl-mouthed weatherman declared. "But you know what they say about middle-Tennessee. If you don't like the weather here ..." He winked at the camera. "Just wait five minutes."

69

Reclining in bed, Dane scanned his brain for a "four-letter word that rhymes with chuck." After penciling his answer, he set the crossword puzzle on the blanket and used his uninjured arm to grab the cup of juice from the bedside table. Mid-sip, he wondered if the hospital's drugs were responsible for the heavenly taste. Before he could draw a conclusion, his phone chimed, and he set the cup on the table to check the screen. There was an email from Red.

Dane,

I'm sorry to hear about your terrible situation. When you're feeling up to it, I'd like to invite you out to the studio for a tour. Though we didn't get to work together this time around, I'm going to keep you in the loop about future sessions. I enjoyed our chats and think you're a great player.

Side note: How do you feel about road work?

My friend Cal has some upcoming dates and will be looking for a couple of hired guns.

I could put in a word.

Best,

Red

In a daze of disbelief, Dane whispered, "No way," before reading the message again. After a slow, deliberate analysis, he threw his head back and yelled, "Wooo!"

A male nurse poked his head into the room. "Everything all right, Dane?"

Dane rubbed a hand across his aching abdomen. "Oh, sorry, man." He gave a thumbs-up. "All good."

The nurse nodded and left.

Laying the phone beside him, Dane glanced toward the window, where twin maples congratulated him with the stirring of applauding leaves. A sparrow glided down and landed on a wobbly branch as Dane imagined how it might feel to tell his family he was going on tour with Cal Walker.

Don't get ahead of yourself. It's not a sure thing yet.

Dane strained to raise his wounded arm, reaching for the juice. As he lifted the cup, which felt as heavy as a bowling ball, Cal's song popped into his head: *"I wonder how it'd feel to be your man."* And he pictured Risa's cartoonish rendition of it.

The tune reminded Dane of pedicabbing on Broadway and picking up the bachelorette party. He recalled his bike-lock striptease and meeting with the girls the following night. Then there was Sutton's blues band, the walk by the river with Risa, dancing in the rain, the drive to Austin—everything leading to the open mic where he had met Kody, who had been the impetus for street-performing, the winery, and all the challenges that had followed.

Tilting the cup against his lips, Dane thought about his smashed windshield. He remembered the savage look in Kody's eyes and the knife in his hand, the sensation of warm blood running down his own back, confusion and panic as he'd dragged himself out of the motel room. Then the ambulance ride—bright, loud, and chaotic as the men in blue worked frantically.

After placing the cup on the bedside table, Dane slid a finger beneath the bandage on his head and poked at the swollen skin surrounding his stitches. Then he imagined walking onto a huge stage with Cal Walker and the band, hearing that glorious roar of the crowd, feeling all that noise being made for them ...

Fair trade.

Peering out the window through open venetian blinds, Dane shook his head and thanked the Everything aloud, confounded by its perfect guidance. Then he picked up the phone to call Risa.

70

Evening roll call ended, and the prisoner climbed from the cold concrete floor onto his bunk. After making himself as comfortable as possible—pulling the thin blanket up to his chest—he unfolded the paper he'd taken from the new guy and squinted upward at the oppressive white light. *They'll shut them off at ten.* Focusing his entire mind, he struggled to decipher the frantic handwriting.

if I'm guilty of anything,
it's living like the animal I am,
by the supreme law of nature:
survival of the fittest,
of the boldest.

and now,
like an animal,
I'm locked in this cage—
confined alongside others who lived by the same law.

The prisoner scratched his head, brushing past his scar.

I want to believe
that we, as humans, are destined for something good.

I want to believe that we aren't just creatures crammed together on this planet—
eating and fighting and fucking,
conjuring rules and religions to
subjugate and stupefy one another,
numbing ourselves to our nature.

Something urgent stirred within.

I want to believe.

but the more I see—
and the more I come to know—
the more my hope dissolves.

and beyond smoky wisps of
maybes and what ifs,
I've discovered an endless nothing.

He flipped the paper.

and in this void,
I think I've found the truth.

Acknowledgments

A heartfelt "thank you" to Sonja Asplund, Dan Myers, Nicole Bethune Winters, Becky Zuckerberg, Victor Rodriguez, Lauren Rasmussen, Rhiannon Ries, Maggie Whalen, Erin Roth, Jamie Hitchcock, and Ben Rouse, all of whom gave time and attention to this project during various stages of its development.

Your feedback was invaluable.

To editors Anna Eklund and Avalon Radys: thanks for helping me to tighten the text and fine-tune the story.

To proofreaders Liz Gilbeau and Greg O'Shea: your attention to detail was hugely appreciated.

To Bruce Rutledge and Chin Music Press: thank you for believing in this book and bringing it to life.

To Craig Eidsmoe (the connective tissue of Pike Place Market): I appreciate your belief in my work, and your willingness to bring it to the attention of others.

To you, the reader: in a world where so many forces are competing for our limited attention, I'm grateful you chose to spend some time with me and my made-up friends.

Cover photo by Travis Tyler (Little Kicking Bird)
Instagram: travistyler
www.etsy.com/shop/littlekickingbird

Cover design by Ashley Zuckerberg & Sara Camille
Instagram: sewhotrightnow_shop (Ashley), sara_camille_benson

More from Alex Rasmussen
Instagram: wordsandmusicbyalex
www.wordsandmusicbyalex.com

www.ingramcontent.com/pod-product-compliance
Lightning Source LLC
Chambersburg PA
CBHW061122100726
47911CB00013B/648